Knee Deep in Murder

A Detective Inspector Steve Wicks Novel

(Book 1)

Norman Wills

Copyright © 2024 Norman Wills

ISBN: 978-1-917129-32-9

All rights reserved, including the right to reproduce this book, or portions thereof in any form. No part of this text may be reproduced, transmitted, downloaded, decompiled, reverse engineered, or stored, in any form or introduced into any information storage and retrieval system, in any form or by any means, whether electronic or mechanical without the express written permission of the author.

The views expressed in this work are solely those of the author and do not necessarily reflect the views of the publisher, and the publisher hereby disclaims any responsibility for them.

For Liz

A truly remarkable woman who

Inspired me to strive to be the best person

I could be.

(1960 – 2021)

Missed each and every day.

Loved always.

Chapter One

The day was beginning to warm up as Jenny pulled up to the community hub in her car. It was warm enough to put a smile on her face for the first time in a while. The weather had been extremely cold for the last 3 weeks with a thick layer of snow on the ground which didn't look like it was in any hurry to disappear and let life get back to normal, whatever normal might be. The Greenacres housing estate's children were just like children everywhere, they loved the snow for the first week but then it became an irritant. Schools had been shut for two weeks but it was proving difficult after the first week for the children and even more so for the parents. There hadn't been snow like this in many years. It was tough on people, especially people with children.

It's said that in the United Kingdom we grind to a halt at the very thought of a snow flurry and it does seem to be going that way. As a country we don't seem to be able to deal with the least bit of adverse weather, not only the cold winters but the heat in Summer too. It would appear that since Covid struck our resilience for life's harsh realities has steadily been eroding away. Jenny was determined to get some of the fighting spirit back and help the community, she wouldn't let everything stop for a harsh winter. What she was doing was important for the community, people relied on the community hub, especially when money was tight like it always was on this estate. Put that together with the cost-of-living crisis, the remnants of covid and school closures all played a part in the fact that people in general were really struggling.

Greenacres Community Hub, in a suburb of Wigan in the North West of England, was a designated 'warm space' where people could come, have a warm drink, meet friends and, most importantly, not have to put the heating on at home. Things were tough under normal conditions but when the outside influences of world leaders were increasing the cost of gas, electricity, food and virtually everything you needed to survive, the people of Greenacres estate were feeling it more than most. The hub was also a place where education for the borough's adults could take place without them having to go to a college. A higher-than-average percentage of local people hadn't had a very good educational experience growing up, in fact most people would not look back at school with many fond memories at all apart from weekends when they could run riot around their parents. Many would suggest that they weren't brought up, more like dragged up and were only too happy to have left with a minimum of qualifications which put them in the well below average annual household income bracket.

The Community hub was originally two large council houses which had been knocked together. To be honest it was becoming too small for the community's needs but would have to suffice for now. The hub had a small shop where people could buy short dated food which supermarkets would have, at one time, sent to landfill. Now it can be bought in community shops in every town across the country for much less than supermarket prices. It also had a community garden where vegetables were grown and also a polytunnel to help with the growing process. Jenny knew that the small number of paid staff, with the volunteers working hard in the background, were making a difference to people's lives and that's what made it all worthwhile. Any success was to be celebrated for the hub members.

Shortly after Jenny arrived it was Dave's turn to show up. Dave was employed as the caretaker and was a very good example of what Greenacres could achieve within the community. He was short and stocky and could moan for England, if moaning ever became a sport, but he knew he was one of the lucky ones and did his job well even though he had a tendency to let the little things get on top of him.

'Hi Dave, did you have a good weekend?' asked Jenny.

'It wasn't too bad, a bit quiet if I'm honest my cats won't go out in this weather so it feels like I've been cleaning out the litter box all weekend. Considering how busy we were last week I needed a quiet one. How about you?'

'Same as you, let's hope it's a bit quieter this week, looks like the cold snap is finally going to come to an end so with any luck the schools will be fully open again this week.' Jenny replied

'My cats hate this weather, it's just like having kids. Can't get a minute's peace. Couldn't wait for this morning so I could get away,'

They were both going to find out that same day that life had already taken a sinister turn and it would start a myriad of questions popping into their heads when they least expected it. It would be safe to say they were both underprepared.

Chapter Two

'Do the honours Dave and stick the kettle on, it's freezing in here and you know that Wendy needs to warm up before she gets any real work done.' Jenny said.

'I'm on it, boss,' replied Dave as he headed to the kitchen to get the day started and make sure the heating had come on. Another cold day outside made for a busy day inside the hub.

Wendy followed them into the hub 5 minutes after Dave had arrived. Wendy was the Greenacres hub CEO and Jenny's boss although Wendy was supposedly semi-retired, they would probably have to take her out feet first in a wooden box before she finally handed over the reins to Jenny. Wendy got straight into letting Dave know what his first job was. No rest for the wicked.

'Dave, when you've finished your coffee can you have a look in the poly tunnel see if anything is out of place.' Asked Wendy, 'I had a phone call last night from a neighbour across the way saying they'd seen a torch light shining in the poly tunnel and just did the neighbourly thing of letting us know, so we'd better put her mind at rest. I certainly wasn't getting in my car in the snow to follow up on it. If he'd got into the hub the alarm would have gone off and the police would have been all over it. I said we'd have a look at it first thing and by we Dave, I obviously mean you.'

'Whoever it was wouldn't have found anything worth taking apart from some old plant pots that we really should have put in the bin last Summer and not much else, maybe a few leftover packets of seeds we over ordered.' said Dave, 'Since last year's homeless guy thought he'd spend some nights in there we've checked it a few times and not seen any sign of him since. I thought we'd helped him out by getting the council involved. He must be really desperate if he's looking to sleep there again in this weather.'

'Like we said at the time, you can lead a horse to water but you can't make it drink… or stop smoking weed. He surely can't have come back to sleep in what is basically a big plastic tent in this weather,' replied Wendy.

'I'll do it now; it won't take long. I'll get it over and done with so I can get back indoors and stay warm.'

'I'll come with you Dave.' Said Jenny, 'Safety in numbers, just in case there's some homicidal maniac lurking. I could do with seeing if there's been any damage done. If it was kids, they've probably put their feet through the plastic. Not a great start to the week but at least it can only get better…famous last words. Not mine I hope.'

As they entered the poly tunnel there didn't seem to be anything immediately unusual. It was very cold as you'd expect with the weather they'd been having and it made the poly tunnel seem like a dismally grey space with benches running down one side and growing racks on the other, it smelt of earth and had a musty and unused feel to it, not like in spring and summer when they used it in anger; wild flowers for the bees and vegetables for the community. Once you were in you couldn't see through the plastic, just vague shapes and little more. 'We'd better have a good look just in case whoever it was has stashed anything they shouldn't have, in order to come back for it later.' said Jenny.

'Hang on a minute Jenny.' Jenny was really surprised by the use of her first name, ever since she'd come in to do the day to day running of the hub, he'd called her boss or chief to her face, on the odd occasion something else behind her back but generally in jest. Jenny immediately knew something was wrong and asked Dave what he'd seen, putting her hand on his arm to stop him going any further.

'There's something I don't recognise stuffed beneath the bench, looks like a load of old rags but I can't remember seeing them before.'

'Are you sure?' asked Jenny.

'Absolutely boss, we need to pull them out and get rid of them, cheeky sods using our tunnel to stash their crap.' Dave took pride in his job and didn't like the idea of people messing the hub around, sometimes he took it too personally.

Jenny wasn't sure. Her senses were working overtime but they approached the wooden benches and bent down to pull out the rags and deal with them appropriately. 'We should really get

CCTV fitted outside, catch them dumping their rubbish.' she said.

'Hold on Dave, don't touch them, don't touch anything. We need to get out of here and call the police, come and have a look at this, there's a bloody foot sticking out of the rags at this end.' When Jenny said bloody, she meant it was covered in dried blood and also bloody inconvenient. This wasn't the first body she'd seen but the others were viewings at a funeral directors, not something she just stumbled upon. Truth be told though she felt strangely excited, an emotion she knew was completely wrong. She had felt for a couple of weeks that something totally out of the ordinary was going to happen at the hub. She hadn't known what it was going to be but she'd just had proof, yet again, that her sensitivity was something she couldn't ignore, she'd been sensitive since an early age. Some might say she was part empath, part psychic. All that Jenny knew was it became very useful in the hub when dealing with people and getting them to open up. Sometimes it could be a curse. Today felt like a curse but her senses were on high alert and she knew when she was like this that time slowed down for her and she saw things clearly, it was like she was Jenny but Jenny version two. That was probably why she had felt excitement, she knew what was coming, clarity was brilliant and she enjoyed the buzz when it kicked in. She'd known it was going to be big but she never knew that it would involve finding a body. That was definitely going to put more than a crease in a lot of people's day.

'Wendy isn't going to like this,' said Dave shaking his head, muttering to himself and going into worry mode, 'not one bit.' Dave's day was effectively ruined already, he couldn't put any other spin on it and within the hour he would have convinced himself that somehow it was all his fault.

'You're not wrong there. You'd better make sure nobody gets in here before the police get here. I'll call the police in, then start letting people know the hub is going to be closed for the rest of today at least,' Jenny replied, while mentally making a list of things she'd need to do in the short term. First things first though, call the police and then tell Wendy what they'd found.

Chapter Three

Jenny made the 999 call and was told a car would be dispatched right away and was asked to make sure, as much as possible, that everyone on site stays there and anyone else should be stopped from entering the property. The crime scene management was massively important and a public community hub building in the middle of a large council estate could quickly turn into a free for all for people who needed help and that's before anyone had found out what was happening in the poly-tunnel. Luckily it was early enough that nobody else had come into the hub yet so they locked the entrance and stuck a sign on the door that said 'closed for the rest of today.' People didn't understand what the boundaries were at a crime scene and others had a morbid desire to see a body before it was taken away. It wasn't every day of the week that a body was found on the estate.

Five minutes later a patrol car with blue lights flashing parked up at the front of the building, 'Better switch the blues off, we don't want to wake up the neighbourhood and have them crawling all over the place to get a look.' Two policemen got out and made their way to the front door where Jenny was waiting.

'Hello, are you Jenny the person who called this in?'

'Yes, I am,' replied Jenny, 'thanks for coming so quickly. I was worried you'd only get here this afternoon.'

'Well, when people ring up saying they've just found a body covered in blood it tends to get pushed to the front of our priorities and the fact that we were parked up just half a mile away helped. I'm sergeant Wood and my colleague here is Constable Bowe, who will start securing the scene straight away. 'Crime scene tape the whole property constable' said Sergeant Wood. Turning back to Jenny he said, 'I now need you to lead the way to where you found the body, if you will.'

'Ok, follow me. I've got Dave, our caretaker making sure nobody gets anywhere near the body. It was myself and Dave who found the unfortunate person. We don't even know if the body is male or female yet.'

When they got to the poly-tunnel Sergeant Wood introduced himself to Dave and put some crime scene covers over his boots and some nitrile gloves on his hands having been careful not to touch any surfaces while walking through the building. Sergeant Jake wood was in his forties, a slight paunch on him but very much recognisable as a copper. Broad shoulders, short hair, calm where others would panic with a 'having seen most things in his time on the force,' aura about him. His sidekick, Constable Robbie Bowe was the sort of copper who still had to grow into his police persona, a little awkward and unsure of himself but he'd quickly 'grow up' in his role if today is a marker for the future.

'So, let me get this straight,' said Sergeant Wood, 'it's only the two of you who have been in here this morning and you quickly noticed the body and called us straight away.'

'That's right,' said Jenny, 'I've seen enough detective programmes on tv where bodies are found and they all say the same thing. Get away from the scene, disturb as little as possible and call the police. There's also Wendy our manager, who's currently letting volunteers and students know that we'll be closed today. No classes were due to start for another hour so we're normally quiet at this time of day.'

'That's good and you did exactly the right thing calling us immediately,' said Sergeant Wood. 'I'll check on what we're dealing with and be right out. Where abouts is the body?'

'Underneath the bench on the left towards the back of the tunnel,' said Dave, 'we nearly missed it. It's covered in rags.'

Sergeant Wood entered the plastic building and immediately smelt the faint scent of death. It was very faint but definitely there mixed in with the earthy scent of soil and compost. This wasn't his first call out to a body and it probably wouldn't be his last.

He made his way carefully towards the body, using his scene of crime training to make sure he left the minimum of trace that showed he'd even stepped foot in the place. He came to the pile of rags and bent down noticing the foot that Jenny had seen. He made his way to the other end of the rags and carefully lifted the rags so he could see the head and try to feel a pulse. When he saw the state of the head, he doubted very much that he'd find a pulse but needed to tick the box as the protocol dictated.

As he had thought, there was no pulse. At that he made his way out of the tunnel and told Jenny and Dave that it was definitely a murder scene so he needed to call the duty officer to get a scene of crimes team here and a detective team too. He'd take some initial statements while it was still very clear in their minds.

'You'll be fed up with all the questioning by the end of the day and the centre will need to be closed until we're finished here,' he said, 'but you've done great so far. I'll go and see constable Bowe and call it in from the patrol car, this is going to need a major incident team involved. He wasn't a vagrant who was looking for somewhere to sleep and died of natural causes during the night, he was wearing decent clothes from what I could see.'

Robbie Bowe was busy putting crime scene tape up when Jake Wood found him and told him he definitely needed to put the tape around the whole building and grounds after telling him what he'd found. He then rang the station to get the crime scene team moving and mobilise a detective team as it was definitely a murder scene. Jake then headed into the community centre to deal with the people in the building while Robbie secured the scene. Dave was left to make sure nobody entered the poly-tunnel.

The first to arrive was the scene of crime team who quickly got suited up while the team leader acquainted himself with what was known so far via Sergeant Wood, who brought him up to date with what he'd learned. With their arrival Constable Bowe was found finishing the taping off of the perimeter and told to keep a log of personnel going through the crime scene boundary and at what time they came and went. Today was going to be very different than what he'd expected when he started his shift just over an hour ago; it was his first time as part of a murder scene having only worked as a PC less than a year and only recently having been paired up with Jake Wood.

Next to arrive was Dr Samuel Lomas, Sammy for short, the Forensic Pathologist, whose job it was to determine the cause of death. A short, balding chubby man in his mid-fifties who, when not in work, was a rather jolly man but he took his part in the role of determining what caused a victim's death extremely seriously.

All the jollity was put to one side once he was at the murder scene. He suited up, got the tools of his trade out of his car and made his way to the body. The body could only be moved on his say so and he wasn't a man to rush and miss something important. The scene was his until he said otherwise.

DI Steve Wicks and DS John Pace turned up soon after the Pathologist and he noticed the inevitable crowd gathering across the street, some in dressing gowns and slippers watching from their front doors. It was no wonder when you looked at what people were seeing. So many police vehicles that had virtually turned up at the same time. A couple of crime scene vans, Sammy's Jaguar, two unmarked police BMW's and three marked up police cars, which had carried uniformed police officers to help with the security of the crime scene and to do door to door to see if anyone had seen anything significant over the last couple of days, which might have led them to finding a body this morning. A mobile crime scene office was also on its way so that the information collected could be logged and made sense of and input into an accurate timeline.

DI Wicks, was a big man whose good looks made a lot of women think that he could easily make a career on the big screen if he ever wanted to. He didn't see it himself, all he had ever wanted was to join the police, and it suited his 'take no shit' personality. He searched out the people whose lives had taken an unexpected turn very recently, to introduce himself as the lead on the investigation and reassure them that the circus that has turned up at their door would be out of their way as soon as possible but that it probably wouldn't be before the end of the day or maybe even longer, but not in such large numbers. He also said he was expecting some more of his team shortly and they'd be taking statements from them as soon as he'd briefed them.

'For now, we need to acquaint ourselves with the crime scene and see if we have a name for the victim. The sooner we have a name the sooner we can solve this case,' said Steve.

Steve went to find John to get his initial view on the scene. John had been Steve's right hand man for over 18 months and their success rate was the envy of most within the plain clothes division. They worked so well together that they were jokingly known as the dream team by most people and by something very much different by others who couldn't even dream about having their success rate. 'What do we know so far John,' asked Steve, 'do we have a name yet?'

'Not yet guv, Sammy's with the body now, he got here shortly before we did so he'll need some time before we find anything out. I'd give him some breathing room before getting on his back. You know how he gets at a crime scene.' John said.

'Ok, I see we've got some uniforms on site, beat us here by the look of it' said Steve, 'get them doing door to door starting with every house on the estate radiating out from the crime scene and when Emma and Scott turn up get them looking for anywhere there's CCTV. Start with the shops over there, the chippy, the convenience store and the post office, we might get some joy with them, then look at houses. Get the uniforms to check if the houses they go to have CCTV we might get something from them, if there's anything that's going to give us a lead let's make sure we don't miss it. Oh, and if any of the bystanders is showing too much interest, get a name and address. If they don't live on this estate find out what they're doing here and tell them to expect a visit soon.'

It was going to be a thankless task doing door to door on this estate, some people wouldn't open their doors to the police because of their previous experiences. Drugs, possession of a weapon, muggings and many other offences meant some residents were very well known to the local Bobbies. Like anywhere you went there were good areas and bad areas, lots of good people and a smattering of bad people.

Wendy, Jenny and Dave weren't used to not being able have free rein over the centre. They had been interviewed but only briefly. Jenny was now, with Wendy and Dave's input, trying to make a timeline starting with the phone call that Wendy received the night before saying there was someone shining a torch behind the centre.

Wendy wasn't feeling great, she looked tired, like all the weight of the world was on her shoulders. She was feeling guilty for not having made more of the phone call from the previous evening.

'Don't feel guilty Wendy, 99 times out of 100 calls you'd be wasting your time by coming in and why would you do that anyway, potentially putting your own life at risk if the person or people were still here. You made the decision that was right in your mind at the time,' said Jenny, 'nobody is going to deny you that choice and if anyone from the police say otherwise just tell them when the last time was that you saw any police doing foot patrols around the estate. If you'd called the police they probably wouldn't have come out until someday next week if at all. They were only here in such a quick time because we found a body. If we'd rung up saying someone had broken into the centre they wouldn't be here yet, if at all. Don't get yourself worked up about it. It's not worth it. Most right-minded people would have made the same decision in your position. I know I would have made the very same decision.'

'I know you're right Jenny but what if we know him, what if he used the hub, came into the shop, came to lessons here, what if he's got kids who have lost their dad but don't know it yet,' said Wendy.

'We know very little yet. All you're doing now is getting yourself worked up about something we're totally in the dark about,' said Dave, 'The guy currently lying dead in the polytunnel might be a serial killer and the world is better off for not having him in it.' Dave didn't believe a word of what he'd just said but Wendy did a lot for the community, mostly unseen, most of what she did was unrecognised, not many people understood that. He had the utmost respect for Wendy, he didn't want her getting upset.

'Morning Sammy,' said Steve from the door into the polytunnel, 'where are we up to?'

'It's definitely a murder,' said the pathologist from a kneeling position, 'but it's early days yet. I can't tell you cause of death until I get him back and do the post mortem, time of death is probably not what you're expecting though...first estimate, anything between 2 to 3 weeks. Place of death...definitely not here.'

'That's not what I wanted to hear Sammy. Nothing straight forward about anything you've just told me.' Said Steve.

'And that's all you're getting from me at the minute. Except his name is Daniel Thomas, apparently, his wallet was in his trouser' pocket so it wasn't a mugging gone wrong. His driving licence is in an evidence bag just inside the door, so we have his address.'

'It's a good start, name and address already, said Steve.

'You might not think that when you see the address on his driving license is in Leeds, Headingley to be more accurate.' Said Sammy.

Steve pondered this news and quickly came back with, 'Great, so we've got the body of a man, apparently from Leeds, who's been dead 2-3 weeks, and wasn't killed where we found him. So, we've got a body from West Yorkshire and as yet we don't know where or how he was killed but we do know it's murder.'

'I've arranged for the post-mortem at 4pm,' said Sammy. 'I assume you'll be there.'

'I wouldn't miss it for the world, you know I like to watch an artist at work,' said Steve. Sammy knew bullshit when he heard it, Steve only came to a post-mortem because he had to. He definitely didn't like it when the skull saw was being used. Not much of the skull left by the look of the poor guy though.

Steve turned, carefully making sure to not disturb anything, and made his way indoors to ask Wendy, Dave and Jenny if they knew anybody with the name Daniel Thomas. In truth he was keeping his fingers crossed that he'd moved to Wigan from Leeds and hadn't changed his address on his driving license yet so everything was kept on his patch. It wouldn't be hard to find out his address anyway and facts would start coming in thick and fast when his team got their teeth into it. Time would tell.

Chapter Four

'Hello everyone, thanks for your patience in all this, it can be a little un-nerving hanging around and not knowing exactly what's going on with all these people on the premises. We are very grateful for your co-operation. I know it's not what you want to deal with on Monday morning,' said DI Wicks. 'Now, I need to ask you if any of you know a Daniel Thomas?'

'They looked at each other but Jenny was the one who answered for them all, 'He's definitely not a member at Greenacre's.' she said. Just at that time Jenny's phone started to ring and she saw it was Patrick, an admin volunteer at the hub who was calling. 'I'm sorry,' she said 'I really need to take this call, it's Patrick one of our volunteers who we've been trying to contact this morning to let him know not to come in, he hasn't been answering his phone.'

Jenny moved just outside the room and answered the call, 'Hi Patrick, we've been trying to get hold of you this morning.'

'Hi Jenny, I switched off my mobile phone last night and only just realised I hadn't switched it back on and I've come in on the bus. I'm outside in the crowd out front, what's happened? What the hell is going on it looks like all hell has broken loose? No let me rephrase that, it looks like someone's been murdered, I've never seen so many police' Patrick said.

'Hang on, Patrick I'll see if I can get you inside the building and then we can talk. But someone murdered, just hold that thought and keep it to yourself.'

'DI Wicks, Patrick is outside, is there any chance he can come inside. I've not told him what's happened but Patrick is an important cog when it comes to the day-to-day comings and goings of the hub. He's the first-person people see as they come into the centre and he also has some issues with cerebral palsy affecting his walking so I'd rather he was in here rather than out there. Also If Daniel Thomas has been in the Hub, Patrick will be the one who can tell us.'

'Ok if you think he can help us I'll let him onsite as long as he stays in the building and doesn't go anywhere near the poly tunnel,' said the Detective Inspector.

'I promise, he won't.'

***

'Hello Patrick, thanks for giving us your time, as you've probably guessed there's been a major incident this morning. A body has been found in the poly tunnel by Jenny and Dave. We have a name and I can show you a photograph on a driving licence, see if you recognise him. The name on the driving licence is Daniel Thomas,' said DI Wicks reaching into his pocket and pulling out an evidence bag. 'And this is his driving licence with a photograph, for what it's worth. Do you recognise the name or the photograph Patrick? Take your time.'

'I don't recognise the name,' said Patrick, 'I don't think it's anyone who uses the hub but the photo is so small and in black and white, it could be anybody.'

'I'm hoping to get a better photograph soon, I've got someone speaking to the DVLA and the passport office to see if we can get a better sized photograph. When we have a better photograph, I'll be back to ask the same question and hopefully you'll recognise who it is.'

Patrick went straight into his role at Greenacres saying 'We're open Monday to Friday 9am until 4pm and we're all in most days.'

'Thanks Patrick but if we need to get you out of hours we'll be calling on you at home, we need to get a quick start on this case but currently we know very little about him,' replied Steve.

Just then his phone started ringing and Dr Sammy summonsed him and DS Pace to the poly tunnel.

'Hi Sammy, any news for us?'

'I've just about finished what I can here with the body until I get him back to base but I can tell you one thing which is of interest. He's had a lot of work done on his face, cosmetic plastic surgery, high quality work too and it's not very recent, at least a couple of years ago. Make what you want of that, it might be due to facial trauma, wanting to look younger or just to change his appearance,' said Dr Sammy, 'I can tell you one thing though, it's very unusual for a man to have so much work done on his face unless his face is very important to his career, I'm thinking actor/tv personality but I don't recognise him. There's no sign of a mobile phone either. It could have been lost in a struggle, which wasn't here and at this point we don't know where he was killed.'

'Shame about the Phone not being here. We can learn so much from a person's mobile phone, it's a big window into that person's day to day life. Everything you've told us about the plastic surgery could put a different slant on things too Sammy. I'll be at the autopsy with John later on this afternoon but I need to get the initial case review going first, get everyone chasing intel on this guy. Let's shake the tree and see what falls out.'

Chapter Five

Steve walked into the meeting room looking calm and totally in control. He knew that this meeting with the whole team including any civilian and office-based staff was massively important. 'Hi everyone, thanks for making the meeting,' Steve addressed his team. 'As you know we're dealing with what Sammy believes is a murder and if Sammy says 'murder' you can guarantee that's the case. That and the fact that he was found wrapped in a load of dirty rags pushed under a bench in a poly tunnel and with a massive hole in his head. The murder took place within the last 2 weeks and at a location which isn't where the body was found. Added to that his address is in Leeds, we don't know his reason for showing up in our patch. I'm calling him our case, until someone says otherwise, and even then I won't be giving him up so easily. What we can definitely say at this point is that whoever did this didn't spend too much time or effort hiding the body. It was going to be found sooner or later.'

'I need a team to go up to Leeds and search his home. West Yorkshire's finest know we're coming. Detective Superintendent Kenny has been in touch as a matter of courtesy but as far as I'm concerned, and as I've already said, he was found on our patch so it's our case and we want to keep hold of it. As soon as this meeting is finished, I need Jude and Scott to head over to Leeds and get a feel for who this guy is, job, hobbies, friends, what were his drivers through life, money, addiction, sex with married women, family, any reasons to kill him. We really need a motive quickly. We also need a better photograph of him if there is one. There is already a two person forensics team on their way right in front of you so they should be able to get finger prints, see if anyone on the system was in his place. I know it's going to be a late one for you but we need a big effort from everyone at this stage, we're already well behind the curve on this one.'

'No problem guv, we'll get his story,' said Jude 'If we get a good photo of him, we'll get an image and send it to you electronically.'

'The rest of us need to check out what we can from the usual channels, phone companies, banks, DVLA, HMRC, missing persons, any court appearances, start a case board and we'll start filling it when we get any intel.

'John, we've got the unenviable task of seeing Sammy in action and I don't think it's going to be a straight forward one. Hopefully he'll be well underway by the time we get there,' said Steve, 'Remember everyone, we are the major crime team, it's not our first murder and it won't be our last so let's do this logically and see where it takes us. Emma, get the investigation room set up and everyone update Emma when you get anything you think might be pertinent to this poor guy's murder.'

Everyone had their orders so they now needed to follow procedure. Something would turn up soon that would lead them in the right direction.

***

As they walked into the mortuary the unmistakable smell of disinfectant transported Steve back to all of the post-mortems he'd been to in the past. He was hoping they were late to this particular party and had missed most of it. He wasn't proud about it but his stomach just wasn't up to it.

'Hello Sammy, I see you're cleaning up so it looks like we've missed the grisly part,' said Steve, 'What can you tell us that we don't know already?'

Sammy looked up from what he was doing and smiled, 'Hello Steve, John, firstly, I can tell you it was definitely murder as I first thought but I knew that already. Time of death is difficult as I don't know what temperature the body was kept in prior to moving to Greenacres. I don't even know when he was moved to the poly-tunnel. Best guess would be 10 to 12 days. I think that's about as good as you'll get on timing.' Said Sammy.

'His last meal was Indian food, if you check his bank account you may be able to get the date when he ate it and where he bought it from, if he was the one who bought it. A lot of it was still undigested so he's unlikely to have cooked it himself, seeing as how he's nowhere near where he lives.'

If it had been anyone other than Sammy doing the autopsy, Steve would have come back with a quick remark telling him that he was able to come to that conclusion easily enough but Sammy was not being anything other than trying to be helpful and get things straight in his own mind, Steve knew how useful his little nuggets of advice could be so he let it go. At this stage he'd take any little gems from Sammy that would help him complete his task and to be fair, what the victims last meal had been could be very useful when trying to solve a murder.

'His general health was very good for a person of his age, if the driving licence is to be believed. No obvious signs of him being ill or any disabilities that I can see. He had a long life ahead of him. We're testing for drugs as you'd expect but there aren't any signs of needle use. Liver was good so no signs of alcohol abuse. Heart, kidneys, what was left of his brain looked good. Just out of interest he had four kidneys instead of the allotted two. I don't come across 4 very often 3 is not uncommon but 4 less so.'

'Could that be a genetic marker to who his parents are?'

'Could be, the problem is that most people don't know how many kidneys they have unless they have a problem with them which calls for further testing. It's not as visible as having 4 arms or legs, so a minor mutation. Most people are buried never having known they had a bank of transplantable kidneys.'

'His ankles and wrists were zip tied to a chair, as you can see from these marks here. So, he was definitely not killed in the poly tunnel, the lack of blood shows that. Find the scene of crime and I promise you a bloodbath. He was killed elsewhere and moved to where he was found. It's your job to try and discover why someone would relocate the body, nothing on the body is giving me a clue why. Need the scene of the murder and even then, it might not give us the answer.'

'Now for the big one and the main reason you're both here. Cause of death was from a violent blow to the back of the head although he had a similar blow to his right knee, with the same weapon, before the fatal blow. The knee might have been a test blow, A very traumatic blow which destroyed the knee.' At that point Sammy asked his assistant to help roll the body on its side so they could see the back of the head.

'As you can see from the damage to the back of his head the weapon must have been heavy, very sharp and devastatingly efficient. It was just a single blow to the head that killed him and

I can say without fearing for my reputation, that he would have been dead before he hit the floor had he been standing when the blow was struck. It's unlikely with one knee destroyed that he was standing though.'

'Any idea what the weapon was?' asked John.

'Very good question John, I've never seen this level of destruction before from a single blow, and I thought I'd seen everything in my time but nothing like this. If I had to guess I'd say it was something made specifically for this purpose. I could reproduce this level of violence if I were to use a long-handled hammer with a sharp, heavy, conical piece welded onto the head of it. The killer would have had to practice swinging it beforehand to become familiar with the balance of the weapon but look at the amount of damage that it's made of the back of his head, right through the skull and deep into the brain. I'd say the killer was right-handed. It's an un-survivable injury, just like a knife through butter, just one hit and it's Goodnight Vienna. At least he didn't suffer after the blow to the head. I can only give an educated guess to tell you how soon he was killed after the first blow to the knee. My educated guess looking at the knee would be within 10 to 15 mins. Maybe the killer wanted him awake and aware of what was happening when the fatal blow was made. If that's the case you're dealing with a monster with a brutal weapon. Find the weapon and you'll find this killer.

The killer must be a very angry person, probably a man as I've never come across a woman who could kill like this and I know some strong women too. You met my fiancé didn't you Steve? Five foot five inches tall, seventeen stones of fearsome woman. She'd struggle to wield a weapon like I've described and she could arm wrestle a lot of men including your current Detective Superintendent Mr Kenny...but that's a story for another day.'

'Thanks Sammy, when you get the test results back get them across to me but I feel like I'm getting a much better picture of the killer now. I'm not liking that particular picture very much either, cold blooded killer or driven by furious hatred. Both fit the bill for now. Oh, and Sammy you know I met Jane, how could anyone who met her ever forget meeting that beautiful lady. I'll speak to you soon Sammy.'

'Steve, you are, as ever, a true gentleman,' replied Sammy.

'I think that's a bit optimistic Sammy but I'll take it, seeing as how it came from the mouth of an actual true Gentleman. Take care Sammy.'

When they got into the car John just couldn't help himself, 'What was all that about Sammy's fiancé?'

'I thought you may ask about Jane. Like Sammy said she was 5 foot 5 tall and 17 stones of fearsome woman. Well Sammy always says that about Jane. It's a coping mechanism, she wasn't really fearsome, truth be told you'd never meet a more beautiful woman, she was truly ageless and a pleasure to meet. You could keep looking all your life and never meet anyone like Jane but Sammy had found his angel. The word soulmate is used too often, but in Sammy and Jane's case it's all true.

I was one of the lucky ones. I spent a good hour speaking to her at some event or other, I can't even remember what event it was now, some police event. When we were speaking it was like everything else stood still and everything in the world was good. Unfortunately, she's no longer with us. Lung cancer, and there was nothing Sammy could do about it. Six months from diagnosis to funeral. It broke his heart and nearly broke him completely. He's doing okay now but there will always be part of Sammy that died the day that Jane died.'

Chapter Six

DS Jude Lawler and DC Scott Hanson had driven over the Pennines in record time knowing that time was a major factor in any murder inquiry and they also knew that the team already had a tough job because the deceased had met his end nearly two weeks ago. The address turned out to be a two-bedroom apartment in Headingley, a leafy suburb of Leeds a couple of miles outside the city centre. Scott made his sporting preference known by mentioning to Jude how he'd been to Headingley on several occasions to watch Wigan Warriors play Leeds Rhinos telling her that Wiganers took Rugby League seriously. He had to get this in because he knew that Jude being a Mancunian wouldn't understand the Wigan mentality when it came to their sport. Jude playing her trump card put him in his place by telling Scott that she used to come to the Headingley cricket ground regularly to follow her dad when he played County Cricket for Lancashire over a 10-year career. Inside she was smiling as she could see Scott wracking his brains trying to think who Jade's dad was.

'Looks like we're here,' said Jude. 'I see forensic lights are on so the scene of crime team is in.' Gloves, shoe covers and forensic overalls were needed so they wouldn't contaminate anything. 'Let's find out who this guy really is. We'll give it a preliminary quick look at every room. The forensics are going to be looking mainly for fingerprints, DNA etc. Unless we find a crime scene when we get inside.'

'If it's the place he was killed it's going to be obvious from the first step into the apartment and there will be a bigger forensic team landing here within the hour.' Said Scott. 'I can't see it though myself. Whoever murdered him would have to get him from the 3rd floor into a car parked on the street where everyone can see what's going on. I think he could have been abducted from his home but murdered somewhere else, somewhere much easier, logistically.'

'Not if it's a crime of passion, but we won't find out until we get in there and do our job. Let's see, first impressions in this scenario are really important so let's get in there and have a look at what we can find.'

'Hi Sandy, can we have access yet?' asked Jude, 'or do you need more time?'

'Hi Jude, we could do with more time but we've finished in the bedrooms, you can start in there first and then you can work around us, I know you're very much watching the clock at the minute looking for answers so any help we can give you we're all working towards the same outcome.'

'That's great, thanks Sandy. The pressure's on. My first impressions looking at this room is that I wouldn't mind living here myself. lots of money has gone into the fixtures and fittings, very much my style, or the style I want, if and when I can afford it. What do you know so far?'

'I would stake my reputation on it not being the scene of the crime, we're using luminol and so far, no blood and I'm not getting anything that says it's been deep cleaned recently and according to Dr. Sammy the crime scene should look like the inside of an abattoir.' Replied Sandy. 'Sammy's words not mine.'

It's a fairly sparse apartment, minimalistic to be honest, but everything he had is top quality. We've not seen any photographs as yet, which is strange in itself. Top quality PC system which we can't get into yet. The tech guys need to be let loose on it. Feel free to get started, but just be aware that there's only two of us here and it's not a job that can be rushed.

'Any sign of an abduction Sandy?'

'We've not seen anything as yet and our initial walk through didn't make us think he was abducted.'

'Ok, thanks Sandy, we'll be in the main bedroom doing what we need to do. Oh, one last thing, have you used UV light in the main bedroom?'

'We have and he was definitely sexually active, let me rephrase that, very sexually active, bedroom lights up like Blackpool during the illuminations. We've also found some long brunette hairs which definitely aren't our victim's, we've bagged them up, and lifted some prints, which we've sent through electronically to base and we're waiting for a name to come through, they may be on the system. No signs of any female clothes or toiletries in the bedroom so, maybe a casual relationship rather than anything too serious. There are plenty of male clothes and toiletries in here but I'd hazard a guess that the hairs we found are female.'

'Right, I was going to say thanks for the briefing but I'm now a bit scared to enter his bedroom in case I catch Chlamydia from a crime scene, try explaining that at the sex clinic.' Said Jude, 'Thank god for forensic overalls.'

'Quick question Jude…' but Jude cut in before Scott had a chance to ask it. 'No Scott, you can't catch Chlamydia from a crime scene, but if you have a condom, now might be the right time to break it out, you just can't be too safe.'

With that Sandy turned round, laughing loudly, to get on with the task at hand.

'No Jude, that wasn't the question I was going to ask,' Scott protested. 'I know,' replied Jude, smiling. 'Sometimes you leave yourself so open and I can't help but put the ball in the back of the net. So, what was your question?'

'I can't even remember now,' said Scott.

'You should be careful about that, you don't want to be accused of premature ejoculation,' Jude said. 'Right, that's enough fun for now Scott, put your game face on and let's get on with what we came here to do.'

Scott had to smile, he was the most junior of the team and Jude teased him all the time but he enjoyed the banter, and it wasn't all in one direction, she could take it as well as give it. He also knew she'd have his back and he'd have hers, if ever the need arose, and that for Scott, and everyone in the team, was the singular most important thing about working in the Major Investigation Team.

They had been in the bedroom ten minutes when they found a photograph. It was to be the only photograph found in Daniel Thomas's third floor luxury apartment. It was a much better photograph than they had up to now. Jude used her mobile phone to get an image and send it through to Steve Wick's email address, at the same time sending him a text telling him what she'd done. It was a photograph of him with a much older woman. She could be his mother or grandmother at a pinch. It would allow someone back at headquarters to crop the lady out of the view and they'd have the photograph of Daniel Thomas they needed.

They spent the next two hours going through each room and bagging everything which could be of interest to the investigation. They found approximately £5000 in cash but no mobile phone. There was no sign of drugs in the apartment and a fridge full of food so Daniel wasn't expecting to be travelling anywhere for any length of time. Any food that was spoiled or spoilable would need to be thrown away and photos of that food taken by the forensic technicians.

By far the best find and the one that probably said more about the victim than anything else they'd found so far was the handgun that had been hidden behind a loose panel in the bathroom. Jude was the one to find it and uttered her thanks for having found it, 'Daniel, Daniel, Daniel what have we here? You've been into something you shouldn't have been, haven't you? And look where it got you...on Sammy's cold slab. It's starting to appear that you weren't an innocent bystander in this murder. Well thank you Daniel, we'll take it from here and this will be a big help.'

Jude let Scott see what she'd found and then handed it to Sandy as it would need to be processed through the lab for fingerprints, DNA and to see if it was on the police database as a gun previously used in a crime.

After another couple of hours without much to show other than the gun and the photograph, Jude and Scott were finished. Sandy still had some finishing up to do. 'We'll get everything back to the lab this evening and let our guys get started on the gun and everything we've found so far and we'll be back in tomorrow morning, hopefully with some answers.' Said Sandy.

'Thanks Sandy, we'll head off now and fill DI wicks in with what we've found so far on the way back and we'll see what answers start to come forward from the lab tomorrow.'

'Ok, we'll hopefully have answers nice and early tomorrow.'

Chapter Seven

'Morning everyone, thanks for coming in early.' Steve started the review.

'Jude, can you fill us in with what you found out in Leeds yesterday.'

'Ok boss, we can definitely say it's not the crime scene,' replied Jude, 'and as the time goes by, we have to start to think that we might not find it anytime soon. We're still waiting on lab results from the forensic team but what we can say so far about our victim is interesting.'

The apartment in Headingley is high end, everything about it screams money; furniture, TV, computer set up, there has been lots of money spent.'

He was a very sexually active man, either that or he rented out his bedroom and lounge to the pornography industry, and before you lot ask, John's already onto that and as I understand he was looking into it all last night...thanks for your efforts in that John.' That brought a laugh at John's expense, but when you were dealing with murder you got your laughs anytime you can. John understood that and was the one laughing loudest.'

We couldn't get into his PC. It's being looked at, as we speak, by the tech guys and the initial view suggests that he was a financial trader. Nothing illegal in that and lots of people do it. I might look into it myself; I've heard that Artificial Intelligence is now making people into millionaires in no time and as I said everything about him screams money.'

We only found one photograph in the whole apartment,' Jude said, pointing to the photograph on the crime board, 'This in itself is very unusual but the fact that the photograph was found stuffed in a drawer means he was definitely photo shy. I'd say there's definitely something off with our victim, some reason why he's camera shy.'

The biggest find, I've saved for last, and it's the one which tells us more about the victim than anything else, was the handgun we found behind a panel in the bathroom. I know we have to match it to the victim because someone is going to say it was there when he moved in. The chances of that happening, to a guy who was murdered, statistically, is extremely low. The gun is a Glock 19, a compact, which is being tested as we speak to see if it's one that's known to us. That's it so far but results should start rolling in from the lab soon.'

'Thanks Jude.'

'Have we got anywhere with banks and building societies yet,' Steve addressed the whole meeting.

'Not yet, but I'll get straight back onto it when this meeting is over,' replied Emma.

'Bank accounts can tell us so much about how he led his life, it needs looking at with a fine-tooth comb, look at regular payments, regular incomes large sums of money being moved, anything that strikes you as unusual. If you need help just shout out. We need to find a motive, if it wasn't for the gun this guy could almost be anyone off the street you might bump into and think nothing of…we still can't point towards a motive yet so we're still a long way from getting anywhere near the killer. There was definitely anger in the method of the kill, this is more than a dispute over money,' said Steve.

'Okay, Jude and Scott dig deeper with the gun and the PC. As soon as we have the PC do a deep dive on it, look for his contacts, his emails, what was his social media presence like, does he have any link to Wigan, was he set up for the dark web. The rest of you need to be looking at motive. I don't think this was a case of wrong place wrong time which ended with him being killed. There was too much anger in this. I know information is scant at present but we need to work with what we know so far. Something will come to the surface we just need to keep digging.'

'I've asked Detective Superintendent Kenny to follow up on a hunch of mine. If it comes back positive things will be much clearer and we'll have a motive. I'm not going to say more about that until we know more.' Said Steve.

'Okay everyone, lots to be getting on with, let's shake the tree, see if anything falls out.'

'John, I'm just going into a meeting with Detective Superintendent Kenny to see if he's got any news for me. I need you to get off to Greenacres again with the photograph from

Headingley see if anyone recognises him. We need something to break on this case. I know it's still early days but we've got very little so far to give us some direction.'

'Right boss, I'll see you later.'

***

Steve walked into Detective Superintendent Kenny's office who ran an open-door policy for his office. 'Hello sir, any news from the NCA regarding our victim.'

'I've just got off the phone with them, very interesting chat, they really don't like giving any information out on anyone on the protected person list,' said Det. Sup. Kenny. 'it's like getting blood out of a stone, I can understand that they don't want any Tom, Dick or Harry finding out but the guy's dead already. It's like some secret society, it's on a need-to-know basis. I think they were embarrassed that they never picked up from our system that he was a murder victim. Your hunch was good though.'

'So do we have a name?'

'His birth name was David Worrall. Having put the name Daniel Thomas on the system it should have sent a red flag to the NCA. His handler hasn't been keeping tabs on him as well as he should have, it wasn't picked up. Someone is in for a really bad day.'

'Thanks Sir, intel on him was far too sparse. Do we know why he was a protected person?'

'Interestingly Dave Worrall was Wigan born and bred, and was part of the Organised Crime Group headed by Derek Wilson. He testified against the 4 top men and helped put them away 6 years ago. He was put in the protected person service and relocated to Carlisle. While he was there, he had quite a bit of plastic surgery done, self-financed, then he requested a move to Leeds about 4 years ago.'

'So, we have a motive to be working on,' Steve said. 'I take it the 4 OCG members who were put away are still inside.'

'Not quite,' replied Det Sup Kenny, 'one was killed inside, Dave Burns, apparently, he got into an argument with a fellow inmate serving a whole life tariff and came out on the wrong side of a shank. The other 3 are still inside.'

'Well, when you play with the devil you should expect to be burned. I'll get in touch with John and let him know, he's on his way to Greenacres now to speak to them and this new name might give us some more intel from there.'

***

Steve rang John with a feeling that the case was going to open up considerably following the latest news about Daniel Thomas being David Worrall and the fact that he was born and bred a Wiganer. He knew that most of the team were still at headquarters so got them together in the briefing room for the second time that morning to give them the news about Daniel/David. NCA had said they would give access to the files on the murder victim that they had accrued since he became a protected person. He needed his team on them quickly as they could hold the clue that they were looking for to break the case wide open.

***

John wasn't expecting an awful lot from the Greenacre's visit. They had a far better photograph of the victim but they hadn't shown any recognition from the driving license so for him it was a long shot that they'd recognise him from what they now had. He got out of his car with the hope that he was wrong in his expectation. He'd soon come to realise that his expectation was way below the reality of the visit.

Patrick was sat at the reception desk 'Hi Patrick, I've come to give you and the Greenacre's team an update on what we now know about the person we've been calling Daniel Thomas. Can you get Wendy, Jenny, Dave and yourself together please and I'll fill you all in with what we've found out about the victim.'

Patrick called Wendy and Jenny who were downstairs in no time. 'Dave's in the IT suite changing the printer cartridge so we can have a meeting in there seeing as how there's no lesson in there today'

'Thanks everyone for your time, we thought we should update you on where we are with the Daniel Thomas case. We've got a better photograph and we now also know that the name he was given at birth is David Worrall. He was a protected person within the UKPPS. He did help us put away 4 people, the main one being Derek Wilson. This is the photograph we found in his apartment.'

They all looked at the photograph but Wendy was the first to speak. 'I remember that, it's going back a few years, there was only myself and a couple of volunteers, Pauline and Eve, who were here then who are still here. The name rings a bell but one thing I can tell you is the woman in the photograph is Karen Worrall. She lives about 10 doors down at number 71, she's only lived there about 4 years which is probably why we didn't recognise him. I haven't seen Karen in a few weeks now, she does sometimes come in to the hub on Thursday afternoon for our cup of conversation sessions, plays bingo and has a chat with the others that come too.'

'That's great Wendy, it makes sense then that she'll be his mother or auntie maybe?'

'She does have three sons but one moved abroad about 6 or 7 years ago and the other sons don't visit very often. Karen likes to travel and as I said, I haven't seen her for a few weeks, but I was also told by one of the girls that she was thinking of getting a late booking to a sunnier climate. I know in this weather she gets really painful joints and a few weeks in the sun does help her, even if it's only temporary relief.'

'Patrick, you see most people who come through that door what's your take on this?' asked John.

'I instantly recognised Karen Worrall. We see her in here regularly, she comes in the shop but I never got the feeling that she was strapped for cash like many of the people who use the shop, I think she came in because it was convenient for her. I don't recognise the man sat next to her, but from what you've told us I've probably never seen him before.'

Dave and Jenny confirmed the same but John was excited by what Wendy had told him. 'We can definitely identify the man in the photograph as the victim,' said John. 'We also know a high percentage of the people who enter the protected person scheme are ex criminals. Some just never seem to be able to keep on the straight and narrow path and end up inside anyway later down the line.'

'Dave Worrall was part of the organised crime group run by Derek Wilson. He helped us to a great result then disappeared like people do when the system works,' said John. 'The fact that the woman in the photograph is potentially his mother and lives just up the road from here means I'm going to knock on her door next. Thanks for your help on this, we'll be back if anything else crops up where we think you could help us.'

'Any time,' Wendy replied, and with that John was off like a dog following a scent.

'We'd better get ready for the shop delivery, and don't forget Dave, if they bring in any tins of green beans, I want a couple for my mum.' Just like that the conversation had gone from as serious as it could possibly get to talking about tins of green beans. Jenny had to smile; every day was different at Greenacres. Today they were fully back up and running, the hub was buzzing. People were learning maths in one classroom, some people were meeting with drug and alcohol addiction specialists in an upstairs room, in another room there were sports massages taking place, people were dropping in for advice on literally anything, the police were in asking questions about a murder and Wendy wanted a couple of tins of green beans. There wasn't much that Wendy hadn't seen at Greenacres and she didn't want to miss the green beans.

John went to his car and got out his mobile phone, 'Hi boss, just a quick one, a relation of David Worrall's, probably his mother, lives just up the road from the Greenacres centre. That's my next port of call but I thought you might want to be involved. It could be the best lead we're going to get.'

'I'm on my way, hang on until I get there. I'll be there in 15 minutes.'

Chapter Eight

Steve and John approached number 71 and they both thought the same thing, 'let this be the break that's going to lead us to our killer.

Knocking on the door there was no answer, after a few seconds a neighbour popped their head out of their front door to say they hadn't seen Karen for a couple of weeks but she often went on short notice to visit relatives in Spain at this time of year.

'Ok, thanks for that we'll just have a look round and check the house is safe.'

'Jungle drums are working well this morning boss.'

'Aren't they just,' replied Steve, 'you take a look round the back, see if you can see anything untoward. I'll see what I can at the front and keep knocking.'

The back door was locked. Looking through the kitchen window everything looked okay. Moving on to what he thought would be the dining room window the curtains were closed apart from a thin slit in the centre. What John could see through the slit stopped him in his tracks.

'Boss, I think we may have found the crime scene for our first victim and we've found our second victim too. I'm thinking it's Karen Worrall, difficult to say for sure from out here. It's not a pleasant site.' I'll make the call to get forensics and Sammy back here and a crew of uniforms.

'Okay, get that started and I'll ring Jude to tell her and Scott to get them down here to help us. Talk about Déjà vu. Sammy will be in his element. It's just become a double murder.'

***

When Sammy arrived, he wasn't a happy man but was professional as always. 'I don't like where this one's going Steve. I'm guessing, without the benefit of seeing the crime scene yet, that it's the same murderer, same weapon, same devastating outcome.'

'From what we've seen so far there's little doubt that it's the same killer. Whoever the killer is tied her to a dining chair and attacked her from behind,' replied Steve.

'I was thinking on the way over here, why would the murderer move the son to a different location, 60 metres away. I'm thinking the mother is collateral damage, maybe to torture the son who has had to watch his mother being killed knowing that he was probably going to undergo the same fate himself at some time in the very near future.'

'Some sick puppy in my opinion,' John interjected. 'I can't imagine having to watch someone butcher my mother expecting the same fate…sick bastard.'

'Yes John,' said Sammy, 'I've seen more than my fair share of what sick puppies have left behind in the pursuance of their final goal and this is definitely on the sicker side of fucked up. Do excuse my language boys but on occasions it's hard to express it any more eloquently. Like your boss said about Daniel Thomas, or is it Dave Worrall now…when you play with the devil you should expect to get burned, or in this case get your head stoved in with great force.'

'We'll make camp back at Greenacres, and sort out the troops. Let us know when we can have access. I'm taking it you'll be performing the autopsy tomorrow morning looking at the time it is now.' asked Steve.

'Yes Steve, the scene of crime team will be here a good while yet, I'll probably be here for another couple of hours but if there's anything I see while I'm doing my initial examination that says I need to do it any earlier, I'll let you know, but it's unlikely.'

'Thanks Sammy.'

***

Steve and John walked back to Greenacres. When the team were told of another 'incident' at a house further down the road they knew, without Steve or John having said what happened that it was probably another murder, they were hoping that Karen Worrall was somewhere sunny and not lying dead in her house only a stone's throw away. There had still been police cars on the estate coming and going as people were still being questioned door to door but if anything now there were more police cars on the street than when the body had been found in the poly tunnel.

'We need to keep this information to ourselves at the moment but I want to get your views on what has happened. There has been another murder. As you can probably guess it's Karen Worrall.

A scene of crimes team is there with the pathologist. We're now dealing with a double murder.' Steve stopped talking to let his words sink in.

'Oh, this has changed things,' said Wendy, 'before today we could distance ourselves emotionally from what happened here because we didn't know who the victim was. Now that's changed, Karen was a member here, she used the hub, it played a part in her life, a small part but she was one of us.' Jenny, stepped nearer to Wendy and put her arm around her shoulders. She could feel Wendy's energies dropping like a stone and tears were bound to follow.

'The guy we found here must have been one of Karen's sons I'm guessing?' Jenny asked.

'Yes, her middle son, and yes this has changed things. It's not what we were expecting to find. We thought if we found our first victim's mother it would put us nearer to finding the killer,' Steve responded.

It was 9pm before Steve could even think of leaving the crime scene and he needed to get away from the cloying stench of the place. He'd had a quick catch up with the rest of his team and sent them home to rest before what was likely to be another very busy day tomorrow.

It had been a very long day for Steve and his team and he didn't feel like the second murder was putting him any nearer to finding the killer. He needed to relax for what was left of today, get some food, not think too much about the case and a try to get a good night sleep. Experience told him that he may be able to achieve one, maybe two of those criteria but he also knew that if he could get his head space free of the murders his subconscious was the best tool he had when working a case, working in the background, making connections while he refuelled with a few beers to relax.

He reached into his pocket for his phone and firstly sent a WhatsApp message. He decided to stop for an Indian takeaway on his way home so he rang his order through and headed off to pick it up.

When he parked up outside his home, he grabbed the takeaway from the passenger footwell and opened the door to let himself in. The alarm which he set as he left early this morning was switched off and the kitchen light was on. He stepped gently so as not to make a sound and made his way to the kitchen, with a big grin on his face.

'You really do think you can sneak up on me in those size 11 shoes?'

'There's always a first time…I am getting better, I swear.'

With that Steve placed the takeaway on the worktop just as Jude finished pouring him a long cold glass of his favourite Spanish beer. He then took her in his arms and kissed her passionately.

'You are just what I need after the day I've had or should I say the day that we've had. Anyway, let's not discuss work until tomorrow, let's eat, I'm starving.'

'Me too.'

Jude and Steve had been having a secret relationship. Anything other than a professional relationship was frowned upon by those higher up the police pecking order. It started off as a quick fumble after a celebratory team drink 4 months since. They both knew, when it started that it shouldn't progress any further but their hormones and desires were saying otherwise. They were suited to each other and both were enjoying this part of life at present. Both knew the only way to progress the relationship beyond a purely sexual relationship was to come clean but they would probably be put in different teams which, in reality, meant Jude moving to another team. Steve was too successful to be moved and Jude understood this. If the relationship was to progress Jude would be the one to fall on her sword. They both knew where it was heading.

They met when they worked in Manchester. The Ariana Grande Arena concert bombing in 2017 was the event which, they would both agree on, made them get out of the city. They had been among the first police to attend the scene, seeing things they never wanted to see, it nearly broke them, as it did with many of the emergency service personnel.

They both moved to Wigan independently and the fact that they ended up in the same team was just coincidence. Steve had been happily married with a daughter. Steve lost his wife and daughter five years ago in a major traffic accident on the M6 near the Shevington junction. Steve hadn't been with them when it happened. A lorry driver had fallen asleep at the wheel and had gone from the first lane across the three lanes, through the barriers into oncoming traffic. The first car the lorry had hit was had been Kim's, Steve's wife, they didn't stand a chance. There were four people killed in total, Kim and Mia in one car, the lorry driver and an elderly gentleman who had just set out for a drive, trundling along slowly, just minding his own business. They were all dead. Steve had been told Kim and Mia were probably dead before the lorry came to rest. This meant nothing to him at the time but after a while he'd agreed that it was a blessing. Steve was affected massively and had been diagnosed with PTSD. He had attended a bombing the year before he lost his wife and daughter, and he was still feeling the effects of this when Kim and Mia were killed.

Steve had considered retiring on health grounds but he soon decided that was a bad idea, the only thing he had left was his job, he would do it to the best of his abilities. Fortunately, he had a lot of understanding people above him and a psychiatrist who believed the job was one of the few things that would help maintain his sanity and give him a purpose to cling on to. He was advised to take six months sick leave to help him come to terms with what had happened but found, even with the psychiatrist sessions, that he was just bumbling about with no direction in life. He was back at work within ten weeks and full time within four more weeks after pleading with his bosses under threat of him walking away.

Steve hadn't craved company since Kim and Mia had died in the car crash. He'd been comfortable in his own company; he had needed the space just to be who he was and grieve the loss of his family in his own time and on his own terms. He had lots of company at work, quite a lot of which he wouldn't have chosen if he was being honest, but more recently he needed more than work colleagues and criminals for company, he needed companionship. He had grieved Kim and Mia for five years now. He would never truly get over the devastating loss but he had come to the major decision that it was time to start to move on. Life was good, he got a lot from his career but now with Jude in his life, as more than just a work colleague, life was beginning to feel much better. Steve had seen counsellors after the accident but all he needed was time, the greatest healer, and a reason and desire to change things.

When they started seeing each other they were both looking for companionship. A copper's life was busy when they were on the job but could also be lonely with unsocial hours and seeing the nasty underbelly of the world. At the time both felt the need for a physical relationship. It started out as companionship but was turning into something more. It was the first time Steve had been in a relationship since Kim and Mia had died. It was a good sign that Steve was ready to move on, it had been a difficult five years but things had changed, he'd started to feel a weight lifting from his heart and had realised that life was passing him by too fast

Steve's older sister, Angie, lived in the Netherlands in the last year of a four-year secondment from the UK. She wouldn't tell Steve what her line of work was but he had a good idea that it involved the security of the UK and its citizens. He'd asked her many times but he couldn't break her down. After a good while of trying to find out what she did for a living he just accepted he wasn't going to find out but was comfortable knowing she was working away in the background. Angie had always been the clever one of the pair of them but instead of going the university route of education she joined the Army and did eight years. When she came out of the army she went into intelligence in the private sector and did her degree part-time.

Steve had lost his father when he was barely twenty years old to a brain tumour. It was not even two months from diagnosis to finality. Some would say it was quick, Steve disagreed, the diagnosis the doctor had told them there was nothing that could be done, the tumour was stage four and had moved to many other parts of his body. The doctors had been surprised he was still with them. He'd watched his father go from a big man, physically and mentally, to a man who ended up a shadow of his former self, unable to speak or get out of bed.

At present life was good for Steve and Jude. Relationships, like life, were a balance but sooner or later they would both want more. Jude was divorced and Steve a widower, Jude had no children from her previous marriage and the urge for a family was getting stronger. She'd even dared to think that now wasn't a bad time and Steve not a bad man to commit to their future. With a DI and a DS salary they could easily afford a good life together and she thought that Steve could move on with his life to a point where policing was not the most important thing to him. Steve was being looked at as a rising star within the force and maybe now was the time for Jude to support him in that journey.

Steve's mother had been a positive influence in his life following Kim and Mia's deaths, she couldn't lose her son too, she had helped get him back on his feet after all the trauma he'd been through.

***

The alarm went off at 6am and Steve unwrapped himself from Jude's warmth. Even though Jude had been awake for the last hour she enjoyed the closeness of Steve in the morning. He was a very tactile man and Jude was more than happy with that. When she stayed over at Steve's or he stayed over at Jude's she always went to sleep with a smile on her face. She realised that the case they were working on had entered a phase where they couldn't afford to be anything but at the top of their game. Someone who had killed two people could end up killing many more having got the taste for it. No force wants a Yorkshire Ripper on their hands. Steve rolled over and switched the alarm off.

'Morning Jude, did you have a good sleep?' asked Steve.

'Eventually.' Jude replied with a smile on her face, 'when I tired of your body.'

'You tired of my body! Oh Jude, that's like an arrow through my heart,' replied Steve smiling. 'It's a good job I can function on only four hours sleep, thank God, otherwise I'd be zombie.'

'You knew what you were getting into when you invited me into your bed, you must have heard the rumours about all the men I wore out in Manchester.'

'You looked so innocent the first time I met you in Manchester.'

'Lots of water has passed under the bridge since we first met, I was young and innocent and you were unavailable. I waited for you to make the first move, like a good girl. You were always the one person out there that I fancied so much but I knew you were untouchable. I must say though you were worth the wait.'

'You take first shower and I'll grab one after you, we need to be in the office before 7 o'clock. Will you take the post mortem this morning with Sammy? I don't think he'll be able to tell us much more that we don't already know but best to be there, keep Sammy on his toes. We'll have the review at 8 am, try to get back so we can have Sammy's initial thoughts.'

'An hour with Sammy up to his elbows in a dead body, just try keeping me away. Sammy's already told me he's doing it at 7.00am, he knows you better than you know yourself. He knew and I knew that I was at the PM this morning even though you didn't until you just woke up.'

Steve picked up a pillow and threw it towards Jude, sinking back into the bed for 5 minutes and smiling. He never thought he'd feel like this again after the accident that took his wife and daughter. Jude was so different than Mia but she was the perfect antidote to allow him to believe he could be truly happy again. Things were moving fast but he was going with the flow and being guided by Jude.

***

'Morning Sammy, how're you doing?' said Jude.

'I'm so pleased to see you my dear, it always makes my day better when a beautiful lady visits, so much better than when Steve pays us a visit. You know you could do a lot worse than Steve, if you're looking for a relationship. Both single, both good looking and both in need of a significant person in their lives.'

'I hear what you're saying Sammy; does the relationship advice come for free, or are you going to charge me for that? You're as smooth as glass you old devil.' Jude liked the banter she had with Sammy and he never ceased to amaze her how uncannily close he was with his advice to real life.

'Ok Jude, I'm sure you've not come for all this advice from an old man so let's talk about what I know already. Having had a look at the body late yesterday I can tell you it's the same killer. No surprise there, a blind man on a galloping horse could see that. I can also say that her son was killed where we found the mother, blood results confirm that. Same weapon to kill them, both were zip tied to a chair, and both were killed in their chair. From blood spatter patterns we can tell the mother was killed first'

'I'm guessing the son was forced to watch his mother die and realise what was coming, that's the worse type of torture. I can't even start to understand what he must have been going through.'

'The opinion back at the station was that the mother was an innocent bystander in the whole business.' Said Jude.

'I'll start the autopsy now; will we be having your company for any of it Jude?'

'I can stay for half an hour, you know I like to watch a super star at work but we've got a case review at 8 o'clock, so anything you can discover in the next half hour will be useful.'

***

The autopsy actually showed very little that they didn't already know apart from the fact that Karen's liver was in a bad way and she probably had a maximum of 12 months left to live. That would have been little consolation to Karen Worrall whose murder looked to be little more than a punishment for her son, a pawn in a game of chess, someone whose life was of little value.

It was clear from the latest murder that the killer had little thought for people who were on the periphery of the intended victim's life, that is if you can believe a mother can be on the periphery of a son's life. Unfortunately, in this day and age many parents can be perceived as being on the periphery of their children's lives. Some parents, unfortunately, aren't even on the periphery. David Worrall's circumstances made sure that his mother hadn't played as big a part in his life of late as she would've liked, the fact that her life ended because of him just went to show how cruel life could be.

Chapter Nine

Steve walked into the station smiling, last night had allowed him to temporarily forget the murders on his patch. He was confident of a result; he knew that no matter how well the killer planned and executed the murders they would make a mistake sooner or later. It was still very early in the process. He had no doubt that he'd get a result regarding his current case. The smile wasn't there because he loved catching the bad guys, now he felt like he had a life outside of that again. He had been scared to move on from his tragedy, he felt as if he would be being disrespectful to Kim and Mia. He was enjoying life again. When Kim and Mia died, he thought he would never smile again.

He was feeling something he hadn't felt in a long time. He also felt that Jude had the same feelings about him. It wasn't what he would call ideal to be falling in love with one of his detective sergeants. He had two detective sergeants and he was happy it was Jude and not John he was falling in love with. That would be so much more awkward, even in the modern world we live in. The modern police force was all for equality and diversity and actively ran an equality and diversity policy but knowing the force like he did he thought it would be a step too far for some of his colleagues.

***

Morning everyone thanks for all being here this morning. Hopefully we can get up to date and see which direction we need to be focusing our attention on.

'Jude, did you learn anything from Sammy this morning at the post-mortem of Karen Worrall?' asked Steve.

'I didn't get to see the full pm but there wasn't much that we really didn't know already, Sammy just repeated what he told us at the scene. Same killer, same weapon, same crime scene for both murders. The mother was killed first, presumably so the son had to watch. Blood spatter at the scene was the give-away on that one. My thought is that the mother was collateral damage, a case of wrong place wrong time, maybe. The mother isn't on our system so although we can't say she was an innocent in all this, or that she was the real target, it's highly unlikely.'

'Thanks Jude, just what we expected then.' replied Steve, John, what have you got for us?

'Thanks boss, I've been looking into the family of Karen, she had 3 sons and a daughter.' John started. 'The daughter, Emily, died 10 years ago by stabbing. The killer was never caught. The case file was never closed on that but the feeling is that it was drug related. It may well be that following on from the recent killings that her case gets reopened.

The three sons, David, Simon and Paul are all known to us. David, killed on our patch. As we know he was in the protected persons scheme and we've found nothing to say that at the time he was killed he was criminally active except the gun, which was clean of fingerprints. Simon, has been inside for gun crime, he tried to rob a betting shop and discharged the gun during the robbery. Luckily, he couldn't hit a barn door from six feet. Interestingly the Glock, found in David's apartment in Headingley, was the very same gun that Simon used to try to rob a betting shop ten years ago. We never recovered the gun but we recovered the bullet. I think it's fair to say that Simon was a heavy drug user. He wasn't at the front of the queue when they were handing out common sense. He's not been out for long, about six months and is being monitored by the probation service regularly. Paul, the eldest went off the radar completely three years ago and hasn't been heard of since. He could be dead, might have changed his name, the list of possibilities is a long one. I think we need to find these two as a priority, they're both possible suspects, Simon shouldn't be too difficult to find but Paul, apparently, is the clever one of the three brothers.'

'Thanks John, you're right those two are at the top of our list, do we know where Simon Worrall is living?' asked Steve.

'He's at an address in Leigh, we'll pick him up after this meeting and bring him in.'

'Good, let me know when he's here and we'll do the interview together. The rest of the team I want to concentrate on the finances of Karen, Simon and Paul today. Speak to Simon's neighbours, general enquiries, what's he like as a neighbour, don't mention that he's being linked to a murder. Jude, you lead the rest of the team on that today. I also need everyone to think about something that for me doesn't add up... Why would the killer take the trouble and considerable risk of moving the body of David Worrall sixty metres to Greenacres and leave the body of Karen Worrall where she was killed?' It was a question that Steve might have pondered during last evening but his mind was elsewhere last evening. He was also aware that having asked himself the same question after speaking to Sammy at the crime scene yesterday his subconscious would be working for him in the background to come up with an answer. Steve had discovered the power of loading his subconscious with pertinent questions a long time ago and used it often.

'John, we also need to speak to the three remaining men that David Worrall helped us put away. I'll find out where they are and set up a meeting, I think Derek Wilson is as good a place as any to start, he was after all the top man in that particular OCG. I'll also ask for a cell search while we're seeing Derek Wilson, looking for mobile phones, drugs, weapons, anything we can possibly use as leverage to catch our killer. It will be interesting to see what, if anything, he's hiding.

'We need to look for Paul Worrall. If he's missing, we want him locating ASAP so we need to look at DVLA, HMRC, passport office and any other places that might help us track his movements. If he's still alive he will have left a trail. This family has something desperately wrong with it, we need to locate him even if it's just for his own safety, as well as him being a suspect in a double murder.'

'Could he have been the first murder victim three years ago?' Jude asked.

'I wouldn't rule anything out at this stage, but I think it unlikely, this killer seems to want us to find the victims. If they don't want us to find the victims they'd bury them deep, everybody knows we coppers don't like to use spades, especially in winter. Things are coming to the surface now, keep digging, metaphorically, we'll get there. Let's hope it's before anyone else dies. There is nothing we can do about the two that have died already, but we can stop the killer killing anyone else though.'

'Shake the tree people, shake the tree.'

***

Simon Worrall hadn't been too difficult to track down. He wasn't at his address in Leigh so Jude called the probation centre and hit the jackpot. Simon was due at his weekly meeting with his probation officer in 20 minutes. With any luck they could be there waiting for him to show up. In the end it was an easy pick up, if he'd run, he would have been arrested and returned to prison. He really had no choice but to come quietly.

***

Steve and John walked into the interview room, the room Steve chose for the interview was less austere, kitted out with soft furnishings used mainly when giving bad news. Steve was going to give Simon bad news but he was also treating him as a suspect.

'Hello Simon, thanks for coming in,' Steve started.

'I didn't have much of a choice to be honest. I got the feeling if I'd refused to come quietly, I would have been on the floor face down with handcuffs on. Nobody has told me what this is about yet. Why exactly am I here?' Simon replied.

'We've got some news about your mother and your brother David. Have you heard from them recently?'

'No, we've not spoken for a long time, well that's not strictly true, my mum spoke to me after I got of prison but made it clear I wasn't welcome in her house. Apparently, I'm the black sheep of the family even though there's nobody in my family who hasn't been on the wrong side of the law.'

'Well, I'm sorry to have to tell you Simon that your mother and brother have both been murdered.'

'Murdered! I'm shocked. Let me process what you've just said...murdered. I can believe David wouldn't make it into old age but who'd want to murder my mum?'

'That's what we're trying to find out Simon.'

'I haven't seen Dave in years, I was inside when he gave evidence against Derek Wilson and his crime gang. I didn't even know what his new identity was or where he lived. To be honest, given the fact that he did what he did he hid himself well to still be alive as long as he was. My mum though, she was the most innocent of all of us, a little bit of shoplifting when we were kids and strapped for money. Only ever got caught a couple of times for it though, a slap on her wrist and sent on her way.'

'Well, I'm guessing it's not easy to see much of people when your living life at His Majesty's pleasure, but we also need to ask you some questions as well as telling you the bad news. David had changed his appearance, you'd be hard pushed to recognise him, lost a lot of weight and appeared to be making a success of his life. He gave the impression that he'd turned his life around and was staying on the straight and narrow. None of that tells us why we found the gun that you shot during the robbery, and was sent down for, ended up in David's apartment... Any ideas why that might be Simon? You say you were estranged from David and your mother yet we found a gun directly linked to you in his apartment.'

'I have no idea how that ended up in Dave's possession. I got rid of it fairly sharply, passed it back to the guy who supplied it knowing it was too hot for me to keep hold of. I have no idea who could have done that to Dave and my mum.'

'So, what were you doing last Sunday night between 8pm and 10pm Simon. Only a few nights ago, you must know that. We're only looking to rule you out as a suspect.'

'Sunday night, well let me see, I don't have my social engagement diary with me but I can safely say with the busy social life I have as an ex-con with no prospects that I was definitely at home,' Simon said sarcastically.'

'Can anyone corroborate that, Simon?'

'No, I was all by myself working on my master plan to take over the world and kill all prison governors. Sadistic bastards.'

'Very funny Simon, it would go much easier for you if you take this seriously.'

'You've just told me my mother and brother have been killed and you're right into questioning me over it. Have a bit of compassion officer I've had some really bad news and being a sarcastic bastard might be my way of coping with what I've just found out.'

'Okay Simon, I would've thought you'd be trying hard to put yourself out of this specific picture... A gun you fired in a robbery some time ago is found by us in your brother's apartment. You're dead brother's apartment. You're not long out of prison and your mother was killed at the same time as your brother. If you think we're being hard on you I suggest you make a complaint. I won't stop you, but my advice is that you should take this seriously because as far as I'm concerned, you're right in my sights for this. So, try harder. You haven't been charged with anything yet and as soon as you are charged it means you're back inside. We're only trying to rule you out of murder. To do that we need to ask questions regarding things on a timeline that we can make sense of. I'm sorry that your mum and brother have been murdered but it's my job to catch the killer and I'll use everything at my disposal to do that.'

'So far,' Steve continued, 'I haven't seen anything that looks like regret or compassion on your face at what you were told a few minutes ago. Sarcasm just doesn't cut it Simon.'

'I've told you the truth and as far as compassion is concerned, I had that beaten out of me when I was growing up. Golden boy Dave was always the favourite and he could do no wrong, mum never harmed me but she never stopped my dad beating me up every week for his own entertainment, you'll have to forgive me but I just don't care what you think. I've told you no lies. I didn't do it. I may not have an alibi for last Sunday and you'll have to excuse me for not weeping into a tissue but that's just the way it is. You obviously don't have anything on me or you would've charged me by now so either charge me or I'm leaving.'

'Sorry you feel that way Simon. I'm sure we'll be talking again soon, but think about having less of an attitude next time we talk, we're only trying to catch a murderer before they strike again and it seems, to me, that someone out there has a problem with your family. Two down two to go. Have you considered that? John, can you show Mr. Worrall out please.'

'Okay boss, come on Simon, let's go.' Said John as he could see the last the comment had landed right where it was meant to land.'

When John got back from seeing Simon Worrall out the first thing Steve said was, 'Get a search warrant for Simon's current address. That interview started okay but it soon changed direction when we start asking for an alibi for last Sunday. We inform him about 2 family deaths and he goes on the attack. I know he doesn't like or trust the police but he just didn't react how he should have about his mother's and brother's murders. At the minute we're struggling for suspects but he's just gone to the top of our list.'

'It's the next thing I'll do boss and I agree, no remorse, no questions as to how they were murdered, nothing but attitude.'

'I still think we need to put a lot of effort into finding Paul Worrall, he's another one in the sights too. I'll put Scott on it as a priority. I'll also ask the question of him being in the protected person system like his currently dead older brother. It seems the whole family is as dodgy as they come.'

Chapter Ten

Steve updated the crime board while John got to work on the search warrant relating to Simon Worrall. He then made the call to his new contact at the National Crime Agency regarding Paul Worrall, if David Worrall was part of the UK Protected Person Scheme, then maybe Paul was too, either because he was too close to his brother David's case or he was a protected person because of something he had done in his past. If he was it would make locating him much easier and would make a lot of sense. three years is a long time to be missing.

It turned out that Paul Worrall wasn't known to the National Crime Agency relating to the UKPPS. That didn't mean that he was still living with the name he was registered with at birth. He could have changed his name by deed poll so that would need to be looked at. Having come across this before, with past cases he'd been involved in, Steve knew there were 2 main types of deed poll, enrolled and unenrolled and criminals didn't always see a deed poll as a good choice.

An enrolled deed poll is registered at the royal court of justice, it's a document that confirms your name change and you can update your records with your new name. An unenrolled deed poll is a simple formal legal statement that you've changed your name. It isn't registered at the at the royal court of justice but needs to be signed by a justice of the peace or a lay magistrate. The unenrolled deed poll is more open to corruption but neither of those methods is actually a requirement for a criminal to start using a new identity. A good forger and you're set for life. Let's face it, the people who know these so-called expert forgers are probably part of the criminal fraternity to start off with.

Steve knew that the right amount of money can buy anything you might need to disappear as one person and reappear, the next day, with a whole new identity. Basically, you can disappear from your current life, relocate where nobody knows you and live life with a whole new story. As Steve knew only too well you could do this many times over the space of a lifetime, all you needed was lots of money and a list of contacts for people who could facilitate it. Corruption paid and it paid very well if you had the right skill set.

***

'John, get your jacket, we've got a meeting with Derek Wilson. Because it's a double murder the prison governor has agreed to facilitate it today. He's at Strangeways, we can see him at 3pm. I have no doubt he won't tell us anything he doesn't wants us to know but I'll take anything at the minute. The fact that we'll be telling him that David Worrall is dead might loosen his tongue a little.'

***

When Steve and John walked into the dismal grey interview room Derek Wilson was sitting at a table with the biggest, pumped-up prison officer Steve had ever seen, standing at the door. It was a bit of an overkill to be honest, it never failed to amaze him that the criminal, so-called, kingpins of the world looked so unimpressively ordinary when they've been in side for a few years. Any swagger and perceived threat had been completely wiped out by the fact that the nice clothes had been replaced by tracksuit bottoms and a sweatshirt, the Italian shoes replaced by cheap non-branded trainers and the fancy haircuts had been long forgotten and replaced by something that had put years on him. Derek Wilson didn't suit prison or more to the point prison didn't suit him, he was becoming an old man at a rapid rate of knots. What Steve and John were both aware of though, was that given a couple of weeks on the outside the man sat in front of them would be well suited and booted and wielding the power he used to. This was a dangerous man in disguise, they were seeing him definitely out of context.

'Derek, thanks for agreeing to see us, I'm DI Steve Wicks and my colleague here is DS John Pace. Have you heard anything about one of your past colleagues, David Worrall, recently?'

'I have as it happens,' replied Derek, 'The prison grapevine is faster than the internet.' I was wondering how long it would be before you came to see me. Steve hadn't expected anything else to be honest, he knew the police force was far from a corruption free zone and someone, either a police officer or someone in the forensic team, could have earned themselves a nice drink out of that knowledge. He didn't like it but it would always happen, knowledge is just a financially beneficial commodity to some people.

'I'm sorry to disappoint you though Detective Inspector, I have a cast iron one hundred percent checkable alibi. About fifty prisoners on my wing and a whole load of prison officers can tell you where I was whenever he was murdered. I must admit though, I can't say I'm not happy at the thought of his life being snuffed out by someone, anyone to be brutally honest. I'm guessing you knew that already and it's the reason you got in your car and sped down the A580 to see me today.'

'I'm not thinking you were the person who killed him but I know crime can be run from inside a prison like Strangeways. You could have put a contract out on him from your cell.'

'If I was going to put a contract out on him, don't you think I would have done that a long time ago?'

'You would have had to find him first; you must have known he was a protected person. Forgetting all that, the reason we're here today is to talk about David's family. His mother Karen and his two brothers, Simon and Paul. Were you aware that Karen was killed at the same time as David.'

'I wasn't aware of that, I'm very sorry that she was caught up in whatever it was that got David killed. I must reiterate that it wasn't me, nor do I know who the killer was.'

'Nor would you tell us if you did, right Derek?'

'That's correct, but believe me I have no idea who killed him but if I should ever be in the same room as whoever did it, I'd shake his hand and buy him a drink.'

'As I just said Simon and Paul Worrall are of interest to us. Simon came out of prison 6 months ago and Paul disappeared 3 years ago. They are both of interest to us regarding the murders.'

'I said I'd co-operate, as we agreed, it can be noted that I co-operated when my first parole board comes up.'

'Don't worry Derek we agreed to your request and it will be noted that you co-operated but don't mess us about Derek, if I think you're taking the piss I'll have it written up that you obstructed us and make sure it's taken into account at your first parole board. You scratch my back I'll say you helped; you piss me off you can write off your first parole board without any come back. So do we understand each other, Derek.'

'We do.'

'Good, so let's stop this pissing match and just get on with it. The sooner we're done the sooner we're out of your hair. What do you know about Simon and Paul Worrall.'

'What you need to understand Detectives is that Simon Worrall is an amateur when it comes to crime. He's a bumbling oaf who hasn't got much between his ears. Do I believe he could kill David and his mother? I'd have to say no, he's always been second division. I considered bringing him into my world, for about two minutes. David put me off the idea right away, said he wasn't reliable enough, lazy, unprofessional and even as an enforcer he would have been a pussy.'

'That doesn't surprise me, having met the man already,' John Said, 'What can you tell us about Paul?'

'Chalk and cheese Paul and Simon, Paul is definitely premier league but as I understand he's gone completely off-grid. I don't know why he disappeared, he maybe got spooked by something, making him re-evaluate his life choices but from what I saw of him I'd put money on him making a good fist of whatever he's doing to earn a shilling, probably criminal in nature. Paul was the brother I really wanted to recruit but I couldn't get him onboard. I doubt he would have turned us over to the police like his brother did.'

'You said you understand,' said Steve, 'what do you mean by that? Has he gone off-grid or is that just an assumption that people are making?'

'I can't tell you exactly what I've heard and I won't tell you who I heard it from but if I were you, I wouldn't stop searching for him. I don't know what he calls himself these days but it's certainly not Paul Worrall.'

'Come on Derek, we need more than that, you've only told us what we assumed was happening, we need something to take away and work on.'

'Okay, okay, he has a team working for him who are as tight as a drum, very professional and very choosy who they upset. He's bringing crime into the digital age, much like the Chinese and Russians but less political. Apparently cyber-crime is where it's at these days. Lots of money to be made and it's a faceless crime. I really have told you all I know now.'

'That's very interesting Derek. I know we are on opposite sides of a very high fence but you have co-operated with us and I appreciate that. If, however, you've sent me off on a wild goose chase I'll make sure your first parole board will be over in the blink of an eye.'

'His brother helped put us away, so I've no problems helping to bring him down, even though I do think you'll have your hands full trying to get hands on him. I'm not sorry to hear about David, As I've already said, I just hope one day I get the chance to shake the hand of the man who did it. Part of me wishes it had been at my request but I can't claim that and it wouldn't be my style to kill anyone's mother. Just make sure there's a note on file that I co-operated when it comes to the parole board.'

'We might need to talk again in the future,' said Steve, 'when we've checked out what you've told us.'

With that the interview was over. Steve and John both felt it was worth the trip to Strangeways. Steve had spoken to the prison governor and it was felt unlikely, given his actions in prison so far, that the first parole board would bring any joy for Derek Wilson so Steve had no problem saying he'd put a note on file, sounded like it wouldn't be worth the paper it was written on anyway.

Steve hadn't spoken to Jude all afternoon and was missing being around her. It was strange considering that he had thought for a while that he would never feel like that again and definitely not with someone who had known Kim and Mia when they were alive.

His initial feelings, when he'd considered the possibility of being with someone other than Kim was one of a dreadful sense of disloyalty towards his wife and strangely towards Mia too. Over time, however, he realised that he would never love Kim any less than he had when she was alive, but he would never have a loving relationship with her again, not while he was alive anyway. Losing a wife and a daughter was more difficult than anything he had ever had to face. Knowing that he might only get to see them again was when he died was just as difficult as he wasn't sure whether he believed in the afterlife or not. Kim and Mia were a beautiful part of his past and a massively important part of his life but he knew he had to look towards his future. He knew he couldn't change his past but he could be the master of his future. He would need to have a real heart-to-heart with Jude and try to see if they had a future together. He would be heartbroken if Jude didn't see their futures entwined for the long term. It was a big risk and would hurt yet again but it was a risk he saw as worth taking, the upside of it would far outweigh the downside. It was a scary situation for him, he could lose the woman he was falling in love with, he might even have to fall on his sword and ask for a relocation at work. He didn't see it as Jude's part to relocate. None of what has been going on with his emotions was Jude's fault, but he felt that he needed to know they had a future. This, for Steve had become so much more than sex, even though he knew the sex was exactly what he needed at times.

Steve had used his police role as a buffer between himself and Kim and Mia's deaths. He now understood that if he'd given himself the necessary time and taken the available help he'd been offered to grieve that it wouldn't have taken so long to feel the way he did now.

Everyone is different though; some people just never move on and others might see this as a testament to the power of the relationship they had with their partner and find it difficult to stop grieving. Yet others might think it was just too sad to be stuck in the past. Nobody could accuse Steve of not grieving the memory of Kim and Mia but now, in his mind, was definitely time to move on.

Chapter Eleven

Five months earlier

Simon Worrall was sitting in his miserable, life sapping, very basic, council flat with his second-hand furniture, Watching TV and feeling about as low as he'd felt in a very long time. This life was worse than being in prison, the only good part of his life that felt better than being inside was that he had more space than his shared prison cell. His flat wasn't what you would call spacious by any means and at least when he was inside, he had his meals 3 times each day, social interaction with his fellow prisoners, his day was filled with work or education and his life felt bearable. He'd expected life to be better after a long stretch inside, life had changed though. People who were his friends, before he shot his gun during a robbery, were very stand offish now, he had no money other than his benefits and at times he yearned to be back inside when he looked at his life and the sorry state the world was in now. The rich getting richer and the poor getting poorer. He could easily get back inside by not sticking to the rules governing his probation. Crime felt like the only option open to him. It really was no surprise to him that ex-prisoners were more than likely to end up back inside, when all they had to look forward to when they got out was an internal battle that they weren't equipped well enough to win.

Simon had been given a cheap mobile phone when he came out of prison so the probation service could get in touch with him. He'd had several phones when he was inside and they had all been better than the piece of crap he had now. It felt like nobody had phoned him, even though he'd made sure the handful of contacts he knew had his phone number. The only people who called him were the people from the probation service. It felt like he was wearing invisible handcuffs, he was at their beck and call and they were quick to threaten him, when they met, with a stretch inside to finish off his original sentence should he break his parole conditions. Well maybe the 'bastards' in the probation service would be the ones who pushed him back inside.

A little glimmer of light came into his life when his phone rang and it wasn't his probation officer checking up on him. It was a withheld number but Simon answered it anyway, he needed human contact.

'Hello Simon,' the caller said, 'how's life treating you, now you're on the outside?'

'Hello, who is this?' replied Simon

'Simon, you really don't need to know who I am. Don't cut me off though, I've got a proposition for you and it could be worth a big wedge of money in your back pocket if you can help me.'

'Okay, you've got my attention but out of interest how did you get my number?'

'Again, you really don't need to know that, Simon. Keep asking too many questions and I'll take this proposition elsewhere and give it to someone else who can help me. Your choice, do I carry on or do I hang up now?'

'Carry on.'

'Good, that's the right reply Simon. I know you must be in the market for some easy money… This is good money and relatively easy to get.' Said the caller. 'You went away for a robbery, as I understand, a betting shop where you fired a gun. Do you remember that gun Simon?'

'I remember wishing I hadn't fired it for a long time after,' replied Simon.

'If you can bring me that gun it will be worth £1000, plus reasonable costs to get it, of course. If you try to get it but can't then, unfortunately, it's worth nothing to me and as such nothing to you either. Are you interested my friend?'

'I'm interested, but I really don't know where it is. I have an awful feeling that this will turn out bad for me. If I'm implicated in this, whatever this is, it won't be good for me. £1000 isn't going to cut it, it's not worth the risk.'

'Okay Simon, I hear you, does £2000 cut it?'

'It's better than £1000, make it £2500 and we can talk further.'

'Can you get your hands on it or is it really at the bottom of Windermere, like you told the police.'

'Do me a favour, I would have closed this conversation down before now if there was no chance of getting hold of it. I know it's only going to be a small chance of getting hold of it but the money is very tempting. So, £2500 plus the cost of buying it back from my original supplier who was the last person I knew had it but that's a long time ago. It might not be out there any longer.'

'In which case we've neither of us wasted too much time on it and you'll never hear from me again.'

'Why do you want it? And how can I know it won't come back to haunt me? I don't have a particularly good history with that gun, if it can come back to haunt me it probably will.'

'It's a risk you'll have to take, but in my opinion a small risk. I have no intention of firing it, you'll never know my identity and let's call it more of a trophy piece for me, sentimental you could say.'

'I hope you don't mind me saying but that's really fucked up. You'll pay for something you have no intention of using.'

'I didn't say I wouldn't use it. I said I wouldn't fire it. I reckon a man not long out of prison, probably struggling with very little money to live off could use £2500. Just think how that could kick start your life on the outside.'

'I could definitely use the money.'

'I'm getting impatient here Simon, time is ticking away, I'm going to hang up soon and you'll never hear from me again. You'll never get my identity so you'll have no way of getting anywhere near the money.'

'Okay, okay, don't hang up. I really need that money. My life is shit at the minute; the money would make it instantly less shit. But how can I trust that you'll pay me?'

'Again, life is full of risks Simon, it's a risk every time you cross the street, every time you go out of your poky little council flat in Leigh. I'm sure you understand that. You took a risk when you tried to rob that betting shop, it didn't work out for you that day but at least you took the risk. I think prison must have made you soft. I'm putting the phone down now Simon, you'll never hear from me again. Goodbye Simon.'

'HOLD ON, HOLD ON, don't put the phone down…are you still there?'

'You've got five seconds and I'm counting.'

'I'm in, I'm in.'

'Good, well-done Simon, there is just one thing I should mention though, nothing I'm sure you wouldn't expect me to mention, as a business man. If I hear that you have spoken to anyone, at any time in the future, about this conversation, I will personally make sure you suffer more than you can possibly imagine and only when you ask me to end your sorry little life will I put a gun between your eyes and blow the back of your head clean away. I won't feel any remorse or guilt at having done that. This is purely a business proposition so consider me a business man who has just agreed a contract with you. Don't ever forget what I just told you Simon. I'll be in touch in a few days so you need to start getting on with your part of the deal.'

The caller had put the phone down at that point. The conversation had taken a very sinister turn and Simon could feel his hands shaking when he put his phone down.

'Shit, shit, shit what just happened,' he thought, 'what have I got myself into?' Simon had got himself into something, with someone he didn't know, but who was a bloody crazy psychopath by the sound of it. He had no problem believing that the person he'd just spoken to would carry out his threat. He really didn't want to be tortured to the point where he would actually ask someone to kill him.

The caller had been working on the premise that Simon was far from clever and more than easily led. He'd been impressed with Simon negotiating him up to £2500 but in the end, money was never going to be a problem. He had manipulated Simon using language he couldn't fail to understand. Violence, or the language of violence is something we can hear all the time on the street, especially if you know where to look. Spoken at the right pace and without anger in the voice makes it so much more of a weapon against certain people. It was clear that Simon hadn't sharpened up to any great extent from his stay in prison. He was still very much open to being taken advantage of. Some people would never learn, while other people relied on that fact. Simon had always been a vulnerable person and it was clear that hadn't changed. It appeared that vulnerability would be the death of him in the end.

Chapter Twelve

In the evening Steve was relaxing in his apartment with a cold beer, lay on his sofa with the fire on. He was struggling to keep his eyes open he felt so tired. The last few days had been so full on and there was no sign of it letting up just yet. Jude let herself in, with a casserole which had been slow cooking all day, the last thing they needed when they were working a case was to have to cook a meal.

'Hi Jude,' said Steve, 'you're just what I need at the minute. Let's not talk about the case tonight, my head is buzzing with everything. We really need to shut off from it all for an evening.'

'I thought you'd like a bit of company; I know it's been a long day so I've cooked something. I was hoping to be here when you got home but it's all go at the minute.'

'Let me take the food off you and get you a drink, is a glass of wine ok?' Steve asked stealing a quick kiss.

'I'm staying over if I'm having any alcohol, so yes, I'd love a glass of wine. My boss wouldn't like me drinking and driving.' Jude replied with a cheeky grin.

'You got me, it's all a plot to keep you here so I can have my wicked way with you.' Steve said laughing. He hadn't laughed so much as when he was with Jude in years.

Steve poured 2 glasses of Malbec and returned to the living room.

'I was thinking maybe we could have a chat about us?' asked Steve.

'Okay,' said Jude, 'I hope it's not bad news though Steve. I don't think I could take that.'

'Depends on your point of view I suppose, I'm just trying to find out if we're on the same page really.'

'Okay, tell me which page you're on and I'll tell you if we're on the same page.'

'Okay. You know better than most people that when Kim and Mia were killed, I was devastated, broken might be a better way of describing it. I never thought I'd get over that but I'm beginning to believe that I can move past it and it's thanks to you

Jude. I'm ready for something more and I'd like to think that you could be a big part of my future.'

'Wow...You're a dark horse Steve, I wasn't expecting that. I thought for a minute you were going to say you didn't want to see me, we'd made a mistake and you only wanted to see me at work and we'd have to stop seeing each other.'

'No, no, no...quite the opposite really. I know it isn't going to be easy with work and we need to keep it quiet for now but I want someone in my life, I want you in my life Jude and I want you to know. I'll shut up now and let you think about what I've just said. No rush to give me an answer.'

'Steve, you certainly know how to make sure life isn't beige. Making a commitment and keeping it from everyone wouldn't be easy.'

'No, I realise that and It's all just a matter of timing.'

'Okay, let me tell you what page I'm on.'

Just at that moment Steve's mobile started ringing.

'Crap, that's bad timing, I don't recognise the number, I'll cancel the call.'

'Okay, I was just about to tell you what page I'm on...'

Again, Steve's phone began to ring, the same number as before.

'Christ, someone's needs to get hold of me and they're not going to quit. It is a Wigan number.'

'Take the call Steve, it might be really important,' Jude said.

'I'll be as quick as I can.'

Steve took the call and listened to the Caller.

'Hello, is this Steve Wicks?' Said the caller

'Yes, it is, can I ask who's calling?' said Steve, 'I'm a little busy at the moment. What is it you want.'

'Certainly, Mr Wicks, this is Wigan Infirmary, we've got you down on our system as being the next of kin of Ruth Wicks?'

Steve immediately became attentive to the caller.

'Yes, I'm her son, what's happened?'

'Your mother has just been ambulanced in to us, she was found at the bottom of her stairs by a neighbour, unresponsive. It looks like she's fallen down the stairs earlier today. The neighbour called an ambulance and she's currently in A&E.'

'How is she now?'

'She's very drowsy, keeps going in and out of consciousness. That concerns us when it's a fall down a flight of stairs like your mother has had. She's just gone down for a full CT scan. She was mumbling your name, and as I said, we checked our system and you're down as the next of kin.'

'Thank you for the call, I'm on my way in and I'll be there in 10 minutes.' With that Steve ended the call and briefly told Jude what had happened.

'Can I come with you Steve?' Asked Jude. 'If we're going to make a commitment to each other we might as well start now.'

Steve grabbed Jude into a tight hug. Thanks Jude, this isn't the way this chat was meant to go but I'm so glad you're here. Of course you can come along.'

'Come on, I'll drive,' said Jude.

When Jude got to the hospital, she dropped Steve at the front of A&E and went to park up. Steve went straight to reception and found that she was still having the CT scan. Just as he turned round to find a seat a crash team came racing past him making him take a step back until they were well past him. Jude found him and sat with him while he waited.

'What a mess,' said Steve, 'It's a shock when you find out your parents aren't invincible. She's only 68 years old so she should pull through, that's no age these days and she's strong too.'

'Stay positive Steve, keep your fingers crossed.'

'At least it's not the weekend so we won't be dodging drunks and breaking up fights, this place is a nightmare at the weekend.'

Thirty minutes after they had arrived a nurse came to find Steve and asked him to follow her. He took Jude's hand and asked her to join him. Expecting to be taken to see his mother Steve was surprised when he and Jude were shown into a small room and asked to wait, and told a doctor would be with them soon.

'Good, when I find out how the land lies, I'll get in touch with Angie and let her know what's happened.'

'Angie?'

'My older sister, lives abroad at the minute with her job.'

'She's not a copper then?'

'I wish I knew, she might be, she's very secretive about what she does. I've learned to not ask too many questions. She'll never tell you.'

Just then a doctor came into the room and introduced himself. 'Hello, I'm Mrs Croft, consultant cardiologist currently doing a shift with the accident and emergency department,' she said.

'Hello, I'm Steve Wicks and this is my friend Jude.'

'As you know, your mother took a fall down her stairs and was blue lighted into A&E. We had an initial look at her and decided to do a full body and head CT scan because there was nothing obvious, but the level of consciousness worried me, she was unresponsive. I'm afraid that while she was in the scanner, she suffered a major incident, we think she had a massive bleed on her brain and we weren't able to save her. I'm so sorry.'

Steve couldn't take in what the consultant had just said. 'She fell down the stairs and died of a brain bleed. She must have been at the bottom of the stairs for some time.'

'We aren't exactly sure what she died of yet but with her good health at her age it will mean a post-mortem to tell us exactly what happened. The crash team were there very quickly and worked on your mother but the damage was too much for them to restart her heart.'

Steve took a deep breath in before answering. When he was back in control he answered; 'She's always been fit. She's never been unstable on her feet. It's a shock to be honest. I thought she'd have many years left yet.' Steve was genuinely shocked, he'd thought his mother was a constant in his life, someone he could rely on for a good few years yet. 'Thanks for letting us know, it's never easy to tell someone of an unexpected death, I know that only too well.'

'Take your time processing the news and if you have any more questions please ask.'

Just then the consultant's pager went off.

'I'm really sorry about this but it seems there's an emergency where I'm needed.'

'Please don't worry about us, get to the emergency, that's your priority and again thank you for letting us know what happened to my mother. Now I think I need to get home and call my sister, let her know what's happened.'

'Someone from the team will be in touch with you tomorrow morning to go through what you need to know to get your mother's body collected by a funeral home.'

With that Mrs Croft was gone, onto the next person in need of her medical skills. Steve felt empty, numb, shocked and even though Jude was with him he felt very much alone. This was not how things were meant to happen after his chat with Jude. He was sure he'd gained a partner, but at the same time lost his mother. Life can be cruel he thought, he knew he wouldn't have his mother forever, that's not how it works, he knew better than most that death was inevitable. He'd expected her to be around for much longer though.

***

Steve had decided to contact Angie when he was home, and he'd had a bit of time to process what had just happened. He'd lost his dad when he was a teenager due to a brain tumour and now he'd lost both parents. Just as he was getting ready to start life afresh after the tragedy of Kim and Mia his mother had passed away, there was more than his fair share of death in his life. It felt like he was becoming numb to it. If he thought too much about it, he would have thought it a worrying turn of events.

'I'll get you a beer Steve, something tells me you've got a conversation with your big sister that neither of you will really want to take part in,' said Jude, 'will you be okay with it?'

'Yes, I'll be fine, thanks for being with me at the hospital.' Steve hugged Jude and said, 'I know this isn't the most romantic time to say this but I have to say it anyway… I love you, Jude.'

Jude looked him straight in the eye and replied, 'I love you too Steve, and I'm not just saying that to make you feel any better than you must be feeling at the moment. The truth is I've loved you for a good while but you were never truly available; I've just been waiting for you to catch up to me.'

With that a single tear trickled down Steve's cheek which was filled with both sadness and joy. It would be the only tear he shed around his mum's death; he'd shed far too many tears over death in the past.

'I'd better call Angie, let her know what's happened, let her know that I'll sort things out, much easier from here.'

'Okay, do you still want to eat tonight or has your appetite gone?'

'I'm feeling famished actually, you couldn't warm up what you brought earlier could you?'

'I'll get you that beer first and I'll be pottering about in the kitchen while you ring Angie.'

When she brought Steve his beer, he'd just got through to Angie. 'Hi sis.'

'Hi Steve, nice to hear from you, even though it's a little unexpected and late for you to be calling…Has something happened?'

'Yes Angie, it's mum, it's the worst news possible, she died tonight.'

'She died? Oh that's awful. I was speaking to her only yesterday, she was planning where she wanted to go on holiday this year, I was even thinking I could take her on a cruise. She said she was feeling really good. How did it happen?'

'She fell down the stairs at home and was unresponsive when the ambulance got there. She died when they took her down for a CT scan. When we got to A&E a crash team came hurtling past me, probably going to help mum, I'm glad I was blissfully unaware at the time. We saw a cardiological consultant who told me mum had died, she said she thought it was a heavy bleed on the brain. Sounds like her heart gave out because of the bleed. It just reminds me once again that we all have a delicate grasp on life and we just never know when it's our time.'

'Who was with you at the hospital, little brother. Have I missed something…don't worry about that, it's just me picking up on everything that's being said and making something out of nothing. My mind has gone into overdrive, I feel like a babbling idiot, sorry Steve. It's a lot to take in.' replied Angie, 'I thought mum would have lasted us both out, I guess you can never be sure of how long you've got left, I always thought she was as fit as a fiddle. Are you okay though, I know this can knock the wind out of people's sails when you're so close to it. It'll probably hit me over the next few days, at the minute I just feel a bit detached if I'm honest.'

'Me too but I'm fine, I think I'm hardened to it from Kim and Mia, nothing could ever be as bad as that…I see a lot of death with the job but this is different. The bodies I come across with work are just that, bodies who I have no feelings for. A crime to be solved.' Said Steve. 'The time from getting the call telling me that she'd just been blue lighted into hospital to being told she'd died was all over and done with inside an hour. I'll arrange a funeral director tomorrow and we'll take it from there. I'm not going to rush anything, I'm knee deep in a murder case at the minute, so I'll have to keep on board and focused with that. I'll take the odd hour or two to sort anything that needs my attention to do with mum.'

'I need a day or two to finish something off over here then I'll come home for a few days, take the load off you a little. I'll stay at mums.'

'Are you sure sis, you know I can manage everything from this end. You really don't need to.'

'I'm sure. I'm due some time off anyway and I want to come over and help you. It's just us two now, we need to be there for each other.'

'Okay, thanks Angie, give me a call when you know what you're doing and I'll let you know if I find anything else out.'

'Thanks for ringing straight away. I know it's never an easy call. Take care and I'll see you in a few days. Call me any time if you need to talk.'

'You take care too Angie, see you soon.'

Steve finished the call and went to the kitchen to see how Jude was getting on with the food. He knew he shouldn't feel hungry after the news he'd had but he was starving, or maybe he just needed the fuel to keep him going over the next few days. It wasn't how he'd expected the day to end but then his life as a Detective Inspector wasn't a normal 9 to 5. If he wasn't surprised by things that happened to him, at least once a week, he was really doing something wrong.

After finishing the food that Jude had served up Steve made a quick call to DCI Dave Greenwood. The DCI was his immediate boss, who had only just returned to work following a 6-week layoff, to let him know what had happened with his mother and to tell him he'd be in early the next morning to sort out any possible logistics around what might need to be done during the ongoing murder investigation.

Chapter Thirteen

Steve and DCI Brian Greenwood were both in the office at 7am. Steve needed to discuss the case paying particular attention to how Steve could lead the team having just lost his mother. DCI Greenwood had been out of the office for six weeks following complications after a shoulder operation.

'I've got probably two of the best detective sergeants, in Wigan, maybe even the whole of Greater Manchester. I'd trust either of them to keep things moving in the right direction while I'm busy on personal matters, it's not like I'm going to be missing for days at a time, a few hours here and there to sort details out,' said Steve.

'I know you've got a damn good team but are you sure you shouldn't be taking some compassionate leave just now? Nobody higher up would begrudge it Steve. You work harder than most and you get results,' replied Brian.

'My sister, Angie, will be back in England in the next couple of days so she'll take some of the load off my shoulders regarding mum.'

'Good, good. Steve, I've got to mention this even though you aren't going to like what I say.' Steve looked at his DCI with a curious look on his face. Have you considered the possibility that with your Mum's death being so unexpected, her fall wasn't so innocent but could be something to do with the case you're working on? A case where a known criminal, turned informer, was killed along with his mother. Now your mother, someone still in her 60s falls downstairs and subsequently passed away, without having shown any signs of infirmity in the past. Don't you think it would be worth me putting someone on it to check it out further? I know it's probably not something you want to think too much about at this time but as I understand, your mother was a much younger woman than her age would suggest.'

'I hadn't even considered it Guv, I just thought people trip and fall down stairs, some are lucky, pick themselves up at the bottom, dust themselves down and carry on while some die before they land at the bottom.'

'You're right Steve, particularly the elderly and infirm. Do you think your mother fits the description of elderly and infirm?'

'No for someone in her late 60s she did a good imitation of someone in her early 50s.'

'Let me contact Sammy and at least get him to do the post-mortem. I take it that there will be a post-mortem. It's a sudden and unexpected death.'

'Yes guv, there will be a post-mortem and I don't know anyone better at looking for signs of foul-play, he's the best I've ever come across. But what you're suggesting is that she died just because she's my mother, I really don't want to think too deeply about that.'

'Let's look at it like this, we're trying to rule out anything along those lines, then your mind will be eased. All we're doing at this stage is requesting that Sammy does the necessary.'

'Okay, she's going to have a post-mortem so it might as well be Sammy who does it. I'll compartmentalise it for now and deal with it when Sammy's given his professional view. I've got to say though, I hope you're wrong about this.'

'Me too Steve, me too.'

'Okay, I expect Sammy will be in contact with me soon when he sees the list that lands on his desk every day. He met her last year and they hit it off. I'll have a review first thing, bring the team up to speed but I won't say what the possibilities are around my mother until Sammy's got back with his findings.'

'Keep me informed of any developments on the case, if you need time off or my support you know you've got it, just ask.'

'Will do, thanks guv.'

With that, Steve turned and left the office to bring his team up to date. He walked towards the review room knowing that his boss had planted a metaphorical brainworm that was going to eat away at him until the issue was resolved, one way or another.'

***

In the review room, with all the team in attendance, Steve told them what had happened to his mother yesterday evening. He reassured them that it shouldn't slow the current investigation but if it did, he had full confidence in each and every one of them to be giving 100%, looking in particular at Jude and John to pull up any slack.

'We can't take our foot off the pedal now. My personal favourite at this point is Paul Worrall, he disappeared 3 years ago but we're being told that he's very much a cyber-criminal in hiding. Maybe his brother and mother knew too much and threatened him.' Said Steve. 'He goes by another name, or several names, unfortunately we don't know these names, or where he now resides. He's probably in another country and that's the issue we have with Paul Worrall. He can be anywhere in the world and run his business just the same as if he was in the UK. 'Myself and John are paying a visit to the National Crime Agency later today. They police cyber-crime in the UK and from what I've seen so far, they're welcome to it but if he's on their radar we need to know. I'm thinking he's a big player.'

'Look back at Dave Worrall's computer and recheck if there's anyone on there, emails, social media etc. who could be Paul going by a different name. I'm thinking though that he's probably remotely hacked the computer and wiped any evidence that he's been there he's wiped himself from it. I must admit I don't really understand cyber-crime, it's too technical for a lad who left school at 16 with average qualifications. It's like chasing a ghost, one that's always 3 or 4 steps in front of the game and can disappear at will. Usually we can visit a crime scene, pull fingerprints and DNA, proper police work, everything is encrypted and designed to leave no trace. I'm guessing we'll need some luck with this one. John, get Simon Worrall back in, we'll grill him about Paul, he might give us something, knowingly or not. I can't believe a man can disappear without leaving something behind we can follow up on. Let's put some pressure in him. The rest of the team I want to look at all 4 people Dave Worrall helped to put away, living and not living. Look into families and known friends, see if there's anyone who might have the desire and motive to kill the victims. Jude, I want you to lead that.'

'Okay boss, we'll see what we can come up with and prioritise when we have a list to work with,' replied Jude.

***

'Hello Simon,' said John, 'we've brought you in today to talk about your brother.'

'Which one?' replied Simon.

'Both, but mainly Paul.'

'You do realise I've been inside for 8 years don't you. Neither of them came to visit or wrote to me, Paul disappeared while I was serving my time. I don't know how you think I can help. I've not seen him or heard from him in years, he might as well be dead, he might even have died, have you thought of that?'

'I can promise you he's very much alive but very, very elusive,' Steve responded, 'unless we get a break soon in finding him, we might have to put him on the back burner and then that puts you at the top of our list and we'll go to all means possible to find the guilty person. We'll turn your life upside down, there won't be anything about you we won't know when we've finished. With your past a double murder will mean you probably won't see freedom again. You do understand that robbery with a gun and a double murder isn't a massive leap, surely. That and the fact that your gun was found at Dave's apartment means it's very much in your interest to help us.'

'Firstly, as I've already said, I didn't have anything to do with murder, it's not my style and secondly, if you had anything on me, we'd be talking about me, not Paul. Crack on, give it your best shot, I'm not worried.'

'I don't think for a minute that's true. I think you're very worried, and to be fair I think you really should be. All this bravado doesn't fool anyone Simon. I know we can put pressure on via the probation service but that's not my style so let's talk about Paul. I can understand your reluctance to help us but you really need to, you're fighting from a weak position, stop fighting, co-operate with us and this will be a much more pleasant situation for all of us.'

'Ask your questions,' said Simon. He'd stated his innocence yet again so he'd made his position clear.

'Have you had any communication with Paul since you were released from prison? And by that, I mean anything, it doesn't need to be direct, it may have come via a third party. You must have been at least curious about his disappearance. I can't believe you haven't at least tried to get in touch with him since you got out, asking for some financial help from your older brother.'

'If you think he'd give me any help you really are barking up the wrong tree. We've never been what you'd call close as a family. I was told by a psychiatrist inside that he was a narcissist with psychopathic tendencies. Paul is all about Paul and anyone else can go fuck off and if he doesn't like you, he'll make sure you don't hang about for too long.'

'That doesn't sound like someone who disappears, narcissists are too self-absorbed to hide themselves away.'

'Maybe he's got good reason to disappear, if you believe what people are saying about him.'

'You said he might be dead, now you're saying he's alive by the sound of it. You obviously know more than you're letting on. What are people saying about him Simon? We know you're not being truly honest with us; some people might say you're obstructing our enquiry. The probation service wouldn't look upon that too favourably. What do you think DI Pace?'

'Want me to get in touch with Lisa, his probation officer guv? Unless he starts working with us, I reckon he could be inside before... no, just after teatime. I wonder what culinary delight you will have missed on your first night back inside. Nothing good I imagine, same crap they always serve up,' replied John, I hope you've had a good meal before we picked you up because I reckon that's it until breakfast tomorrow.'

'Okay, okay, I've heard he's not dead, he just doesn't want to be found,' replied Simon.

'And why doesn't he want to be found Simon?' Asked Steve.

'I imagine he's rolling around in ill-gotten gains like a pig in shit, that's my best guess but you'll really have to ask him yourself.'

'We'd love to, but we can't find him.'

'Well, DI Wicks, that's not my problem, is it? I'm just as incapable of reaching him as much as you are.'

'Let me ask the question again. Have you had any communication with your brother Paul since you got out of prison, anything at all, do you know anybody who has?'

'No I don't, if I had I'd tell you.'

'Who was it who told you Paul was definitely alive? Give us a name Simon, and if I find out you're lying you'll be back inside and your feet won't touch the ground.'

'Oh, that one I can do, her name was Karen Worrall, the same Karen Worrall who's now lay in the morgue, the same Karen

Worrall who had basically disowned me when I came out of prison. Fill your boots fellas, be my guest.' said Simon.

'That's convenient, for you. A little too convenient if you ask me.'

'Listen, if I could hand you my brother Paul on a plate I really would. He always saw himself as too good for the likes of me, he was too good for most people, he has a lot of enemies. My brother has a knack of attracting them, as I've already said, Paul is all about Paul. He was never a very friendly person, any relationships he had didn't last long. As soon as people got to know him, they moved away, quickly. Do I think he's capable of killing my mum and Dave? Yes, I do.'

'Any criminal associates who might know where he is or the name he goes by these days?'

'None that would give you the time of day, but that's no big shock there is it? Look what happened to Dave, he talked to you lot and ended up dead and if you turn up at their door, they'll be looking for someone to blame and they'd not have to look very far to blame me. So on this occasion gentlemen I'll have to respectfully decline.'

'Okay Simon, don't go travelling too far, I'm sure we'll be speaking again soon.'

'Where would I go, really?'

'All we're getting off you Simon is how shit your life is. It was you who made your choices in life though, nobody else. But let's face it you're still doing better than your Dave and your mum.'

'Am I though, I really am beginning to wonder, job prospects…nil, real friends…nil, financial security…nil, family…rapidly disappearing, living in a shithole…absolutely. Not that it matters to anyone other than me.'

'Some people come out of prison having learned an important lesson. It's time you learned that important lesson Simon. You set yourself up for this life and only you can improve your lot. If you don't, you're going straight back inside. As I said don't travel far, we'll be speaking to you again, soon.' With that last nugget of wise words, the interview was over and Simon Worrall was sent on his way.

'I don't think he has it in him to have murdered anybody to be honest, what do you think John?'

'I'm coming to the same conclusion guv, he's got a big down on himself, the guy's head is so messed up and bitter but I think he's more pissed off with himself than anyone else…Even if he was ever feeling murderous, I don't think he's got it in him.'

Chapter Fourteen

Steve woke up, alone, feeling low which wasn't like Steve, he was generally an upbeat person; it paid dividends in his job but he felt like he was getting nowhere fast and struggling to get a worthy lead. It might have been that he had been on his own the previous night and subsequently he was up most of the night running scenarios in his head instead of sleeping. His experience told him that cases do sometimes take a while to break so he put his mood down to missing the warmth of Jude in his bed.

He needed to speak to the NCA about cyber-crime and although it needed to be done it would feel like he was losing control of the case, not that he was getting anywhere when he is in control.

When he got into the station, the first thing he did was search out Jude to ask how things had gone the previous day.

He found Jude in the corridor and took her a good distance from the nearest office. 'Hi Jude, how did the computer search go yesterday?' Asked Steve. 'Missed you last night by the way, I was lonely.'

'Computer search hasn't revealed anything as yet but I'm still on it. Missed you too, you big lump, I'll be there tonight though, don't fret, I was tired last night, I won't be tonight, big man,' replied Jude, with a big grin on her face.

'Can't wait... but in the meantime, can you get information on all 4 of the men Dave Worrall, helped put away, Derek Wilson, Bill Davis, Jonny Stevens and Dave Burns, see if there's anything that jumps out, and also let's see if we can get a list together of any foreign travel that Karen Worrall has done over the last 3 years, see if there's any patterns and who paid for the tickets. Apparently, Paul Worrall was the golden child and maybe he funded his mother's foreign travel to visit him.'

'Will do, guv.'

***

Steve and John had left Jude in charge of collecting intel. Get your jacket John, we're going to the NCA cyber-crime unit to see if they can help us with locating Paul Worrall.

'We could really use a break on this one guv, everywhere we turn we seem to come up against a brick wall.'

They were met at the NCA reception by Mark Green and taken through to an office. 'The security around here is a step up from our offices at Wigan,' said Steve.

'Yes, it is, when you're dealing with cyber-crime it's not only physically getting into and out of the building. We've also got government approved protocols around anything we do electronically. How can we help you; I believe it's got something to do with cyber,' said Mark.

'We're working a double murder case at the minute and we'd like to locate and get our hands on the brother of one of the deceased, son of the other,' replied Steve. 'We believe he's running a cyber-crime gang, probably not in this country and definitely using a false name. His birth name is Paul Worrall, are you familiar with him?'

'Very familiar with him, he's a person who really interests us. He isn't a small-time player, that's why we're so interested in him, very professional, and if he's done what we believe he's done he's very profitable too. He moves around from country to country, sets up in empty factory units on quiet industrial units, in the middle of nowhere, uses it for a small time then moves on. By the time we get anywhere near him he's moved on. So far, we know he's been in Scotland, France, Greece, Poland and Russia to name a few. Always pays his bills on time, never anything but a perfect tenant. Every route we go down to get near him is a dead end. He's that good.'

'Consider us both cyber amateurs. Can you tell us the types of crimes he and his gang might be committing,' asked Steve.

'It's a faceless crime, all done in the ether. There are lots of ways he can get money from a dear old granny, who is more and more being forced to use a computer to do her shopping online right up to major corporations who have data stolen. Because of the consequences to their clients they are often willing to pay a ransom to the criminals to make the criminals go away. The bigger the organisation the bigger the ransom demand,' replied Mark.

'So explain how it works.'

'Talking legislatively, the computer misuse act 1990 states that people can be prosecuted if they gain unauthorised access to a computer's data and sensitive information with malicious intent and without permission. The intentional use of computers to commit a crime or harm others. There was a recent case regarding the Police Service of Northern Ireland where the identities of all police officers in Northern Ireland were leaked online. This is a very serious issue, as people think all the problems with the violence in Northern Ireland has gone away. This is very much not the case. Lots of police officers in Northern Ireland don't even tell their families that they're police officers.'

'I can see why that would be a problem.' Replied Steve.

'Basically the way this started was with hacking, gaining unauthorised access to a computer system. When they're in a computer they can steal sensitive information, install software, even wipe all the data. Then there's Malware, malicious software such as viruses, ransomware, keyloggers.'

'Keyloggers, that's a new one on me,' Steve said.

'Keyloggers steal passwords for credit cards, basically they log any keypad usage.'

'God, that's frightening, it's a bit big brother watching over everyone.'

'Watching and stealing as they go.'

'Another one is a denial of service or DOS attack where someone crashes the site. There are many scams that can be run by organisations big or small. Dating and romance scams, holiday fraud, ticketing scams, online shopping scams. The list is big and getting bigger all the time, I've just scratched the surface. People become blasé about computer fraud. It's an it'll never happen to me mindset it's not happened so far so it'll not happen in the future. All that means is they've been lucky so far.'

'You make it sound like cyber-criminals have an endless supply of money to dip into. Is it really that simple? Asked Steve.

'Unfortunately, the answer to that is yes, it's like throwing a big fishing net into the sea, sometimes you come out with a few mackerel and at other times you land a full net. Throw the net into the sea enough times and you'll end up a rich man.

'So how, exactly, do we get our hands on Paul Worrall to interview him with regards to the double murder. It seems that anyone in cyber-crime is expert at dodging the law.'

'I really don't want to put a dampener on your chances but if I tell you the Pentagon and Nasa were both hacked by a guy, sat in his bedroom in England, looking for proof that aliens exist. He spent enough time in their system to get proof positive, apparently. Now, you're talking about a gang of well organised criminals, highly motivated and highly mobile, who we haven't got anywhere near in 3 years…well it gives you an idea of the severity of your problem. We'll red flag him on our system and we'll make sure he's moved up the priority list but as I've said, the organised gangs are usually 3 or 4 moves ahead of law enforcement. Don't think he doesn't know you're coming for him either. He'll know exactly who you are and, if he has a mind to, he'll empty your bank account in the blink of an eye, just to piss you off.'

If Steve was feeling down about how things were working out when he woke up this morning, he was now feeling so much worse.

'Bloody hell guv, I feel like slashing at my wrists after that meeting. He was brutal,' said John in the car, on the drive back to Wigan.

'I think it must be a really tough job to make you that despondent. Maybe he was just being honest from his experience. It doesn't help us get any closer to Paul Worrall, or whatever name he's going by this week, though. It's not very often I get stuck on a problem like this. I can usually come up with some strategy to get us moving forward but I'll hold my hands up, I'm struggling. Hopefully Jude has dug out some intel that's a bit more positive.'

When they arrived back at the station Steve and John went directly to the incident room.

'Please tell me you've got some good news for me Jude,' said Steve who was frustrated by his meeting with Mark Green at NCA.

'Well, I've got news,' said Jude, 'I think it's good but I'll let you decide that. We've been concentrating on Karen Worrall's travel since her elusive son disappeared off the radar. It turns out she's really well travelled for a single elderly woman. Luckily for us she used one travel agent for every trip she made. That made the task easier for us than if it had been random. You've got to love elderly people and their unwillingness to change something when it works.'

'Great Jude what have you found out?'

'She travelled in Europe, which isn't too unusual, she visited Spain, Germany, Poland twice, Greece, Lithuania twice, Belarus and once just over the border into Russia in that order' Replied Jude. 'Now that's an awful lot of travel for a woman her age, travelling alone and some of those countries wouldn't necessarily be on the list of countries I'd want to visit if I was in her position. One more thing which I found interesting was the two visits to Lithuania and two visits to Poland, were made one after the other, as if she was meeting visiting someone there, maybe, who happened to be in those countries longer than usual.'

'That's exactly how I see it too, have you got a list together with dates and how long she was away for?'

'Yes, I'm just putting the finishing touches to it to it now, give me 10 minutes and I'll have it on your desk.'

'John, when we get that list, we need to get it over to Mark Green at the NCA then we'll set up a joint call with him to let him know we think we might have a list of countries Paul Worrall was operating from and dates when we think he might have been in those countries with his mother. I think Europol need to be included in this at some time in the near future.'

'Will do guv, do you want me to set up the call now or tomorrow morning?' said John.

Looking at his watch, Steve made the decision to get it set up for tomorrow morning at 9am.

'Just one more thing guv,' said Jude, she had a trip scheduled in 3 weeks to Spain, so he might be in Spain now or due in Spain within the next few weeks, maybe we can get a link into the airport arrivals lounge, see if anyone we can recognise turns up to meet her.'

'Great work Jude, let's keep that one under our hat for now. What would be useful though is to find out who was paying for these trips, herself or somebody else.'

'We're already looking at that guv, I'll make sure it's added to the list shortly. She had enough money in her bank account to pay for herself, much more than we'd expect someone on the Greenacre estate to have.'

'When you've got three sons who have been, or still are, involved in criminal activity and two out of those three are apparently successful, either legally or illegally, it wouldn't surprise me to learn that. If the mountain won't come to Muhammad, then Muhammad must go to the mountain, or to put it another way, if Paul can't come to visit his mother, then his mother must go to Paul, no matter where that might be. It's no wonder little brother Simon has got such a big chip on his shoulder. See if you can tie David Worrall into any of those trips. Great work Jude. I must admit I felt like all we were coming up against was brick walls, now I feel like we've just knocked over a wall. Next thing we need to get the team looking at is family and friends of the four people David Worrall helped us put inside, the three currently living and the one that was murdered inside. I'm actually thinking definitely the one that was murdered inside, purely for the reason that he shares something with our two victims. They're all dead.'

Chapter Fifteen

Back at home and feeling much better about the case Steve relaxed with Jude by his side. That day's work had been neatly packed away to the back of his mind until tomorrow. A copper's working day was never really ended, especially when you get to the level of detective inspector.

The first thing that happened was Sammy calling him to give him his condolences for his mother, Ruth. He also mentioned the fact that DCI Dave Greenwood had called him to make sure he was the one doing his mother's post-mortem tomorrow morning and that he would ensure the utmost respect was given.

'I know that, Sammy, you don't have to say it. I'm glad it's yourself doing it, I know how you work I know you'll give her respect, like you give to everyone who comes into your workplace. I never even considered that we'd be having this conversation. The fact that she might have been pushed down the stairs might mean we're getting close to whoever killed the Worrall's. It doesn't feel like it.' Said Steve. 'Thanks for calling Sammy, I really appreciate it.'

'I'll send you the report as soon as it's ready. Don't worry Steve, she's in good hands.'

With that Steve rang off and getting up he asked Jude if she fancied a cold beer.

'Oh, yes please, we're in for the night so I'd love one,' replied Jude.

Two minutes later Steve's mobile received a text message from a number he didn't recognise. 'I hope this isn't anything to do with work,' said Jude.

Steve read the text to himself then read it aloud to Jude.

'You're not going to believe this Jude, listen to this... Detective inspector Wicks, I believe you have an urgent need to speak to me regarding the untimely deaths of my mother and brother. As I'm sure you understand, by now, I have no desire to speak to you face-to-face. I'm not in the UK now and haven't been for some time. I may never be back in the UK again. The weather is so much better where I'm texting from and I have very little desire to come back to a country where I'd be putting my liberty at risk. You can try to trace me through this message; however, I can promise you though, that all you'll find is a brick wall in your path. I can tell you I had nothing to do with my mother's and brother's deaths. If you have any questions for me, put them in an email to yourself and I'll have a look at them tomorrow… Say hi to Detective Sergeant Lawler for me, Jude Lawler. I don't know her, but having been in your phone for the last 30 minutes, I feel like I've known her for years…All this hiding from consequences, it appears we aren't very different after all…Paul W.'

'What the hell! How does he know about us? Bare faced cheek of the man!' exclaimed Jude.

'He's had a good look at my phone, good job I don't use it for any work stuff. He's obviously been in my emails and text messages. I don't believe this guy,' said Steve. 'At least he's just proved to us that he's still alive.'

'You need to let NCA see that. Take a screenshot of it.'

'Ok, just done it.'

Steve went back to look at the message, 'He's taken the message down already, it's no longer there, on the face of it, it's like I never received it.' Steve then went into his screenshot folder, it was empty. 'Jesus Jude he's wiped clean every screenshot I had stored on this piece of shit phone.'

'Is that your personal phone or your work phone?'

'Personal.'

'Turn it off, now. We need to get it to our tech guys, let them have a look at it,' said Jude.

'You've got to wonder why he would start communicating with me though. If he is our killer, he'd surely stay well away, instead he's just given us a potential way in.

'I think he's too clever to give us a way in to be honest,' said Jude, 'not an easy one anyway.'

'He's playing with us,' said Steve looking at his phone, I got a screenshot of the message but didn't even get a chance to look at it before he wiped it away. He's got some serious skills, and he's using them to take the piss out of us, that's what it feels like.'

'Who told him we want to speak with him? How did he know you're the lead on the case? Who told him your personal phone number? I could probably make a long list of people who could have told him but they'd have to be good. We've got a team working on trying to find him and we haven't really got anywhere near him. Have we got a mole who knows how to contact him? It has to be an insider.' Jude was feeling as frustrated as Steve.

'Same day John and I paid a visit to the NCA, seems like a hell of a coincidence. Can we trust the NCA with this? I'm feeling technically inadequate to be honest. I'm suddenly feeling out of my depth. This must be how old people feel. It's no wonder cyber-crime is so hot. It really must be like taking candy from a baby.'

'I'll contact our tech guys, there won't be many people in but I'm guessing the boffins must be covering the night shift.' Five minutes later Jade came off the phone and spoke to Steve.

'There's a rush job that needs to be done tonight and they're one down to sickness. If we took it in tonight, they might not even get a chance to give it a cursory glance. They said to keep it switched off and bring it in first thing tomorrow when there should be a full complement in. He said it sounds like the guy who did it is so far ahead of us in cyber terms that he's in a different league. Why do men always like a sporting analogy?'

'It's just the way our brains are wired, but it's always the case in sport that a second division team can beat a premier league team on their day. We just need the break and we'll get this one sorted,' replied Steve, 'my phone's off for now and we'll speak to our tech guys tomorrow, let them deconstruct it if necessary. I think only after our guys have looked at it will we think about the NCA having a look. I might take some advice on that one, considering we visited them on the same day Paul Worrall decided to contact me. Maybe he's already in their system and they don't know it yet. This isn't something we come across very often and I'm pretty sure telling the NCA that they've been hacked or have a mole is way out of my pay scale. So for tonight I'm going to compartmentalise it, lock it away for a few hours and pick it up again tomorrow morning.'

'Fancy that drink now, Steve?' asked Jude. 'I need something a bit stronger than a beer. I'm thinking red wine, I'll get it, what about you? Red wine?'

'Yes, I'm with you, need one, red wine sounds just about right. How about cheese and crackers too?' asked Steve.

'Perfect. Thanks Steve.' Jude followed Steve into the kitchen, 'I've just had a thought; Paul Worrall could make out our relationship from your phone and you're going to give the same phone to our tech team.'

'Don't worry about that, it has to come out at some stage. I'm not embarrassed by our relationship and I don't think you are either; I'll shout it out from the top step of the town hall if I need to. Let's see what happens, we're not the first coppers to fall for each other.'

'I might keep you to that…the town hall steps thing. It might blow a few minds but work isn't going to break us up.'

'Not a chance.'

Steve went straight to the tech team in the basement first thing the next morning. Jude had agreed to follow him in twenty minutes later. If they were going to come out of this with jobs intact, they needed to keep up the pretence, for a little longer at least.

'Hi Tony,' said Steve, Tony was expecting him to drop his phone off. 'That coffee always smells so nice when I come in here. I wish I could stay and get a nice dose of caffeine but my personal mobile phone was hacked last night by one of our main suspects in a double murder case. Brother to one of the victims, son to the other. His name is Paul Worrall although he doesn't go by that name now. He lives abroad and as we understand he's the leader of a well organised crime gang, cybercrime to be more precise. Basically he sent me a text message last night and when I'd read it a couple of times he removed it and any evidence of it from my phone and deleted all my screenshots too just in case. I actually think he was just flexing his cyber muscles, letting me know he's no amateur. What I need is for you guys to see if he's left any clues behind. I then need you to copy all my files, emails, text messages and anything else on there which isn't anything to do with text messages from last night. I basically want a clean phone onto which I can leave a message for him to pick up at his leisure. Can that be done?'

'Of course it can, I'll do it myself. The guy sounds very confident of his abilities,' replied Tony.

'He is, and from what I saw last night he has good reason to be. You can get me on my police issue phone. I'm taking that that is better protected than my personal mobile?'

'It is, we've got many levels of protection pointed at those phones at all levels. It's expensive and isn't a guarantee that a hacker won't bypass the security…given time, the difference is we'd know he's there if he got in.'

'Okay, that's reassuring. Oh and Tony it's my personal phone so no digging too deep into what's on there…and no, I'm not a fully paid-up member of several fetish porn sites. There are sensitive communications that if leaked will lead me directly back to your door or the suspected murderer.'

'Understood Steve, nothing will come from me, even if I do stumble across anything I shouldn't. I'll be a beacon of discretion,' replied Tony.

'Good man Tony, don't let the phone out of your sight.'

'Don't worry, I'll treat it like it's one of my daughters. I'll be in touch later.'

'Cheers mate, see you later.'

Next stop for Steve would be DCI Greenwood's office to explain that Paul Worrall had been in touch and the suspect, unfortunately, was the one pulling all the strings.

'Okay Steve, I think you've done the right thing disinfecting your phone of everything apart from the text message app. It's far from ideal but if he knows anything he might be able to give us a good lead to take the heat off himself.' Said DCI Greenwood

'I've got to say Guv, the thing that's really making alarm bells ring is that yesterday myself and John went to see the NCA for a meeting regarding Paul Worrall's cybercrime career. It was only a few hours after that when Paul Worrall got in touch with me. It feels like too much of a coincidence to me but to be honest with you I do feel out of my depth with the cyber aspect of this case. It really surprised me what a clever guy, with a computer and systems to protect himself, is capable of. It's scary.

'Thanks for bringing it to my attention Steve. I'll have a think about the NCA situation, maybe even take it upstairs to discuss it with Superintendent Kenny.'

'Thanks Guv, I'll update my team soon and see where we're at. I'll keep you updated, like you say, a guy like Paul Worrall may be more than happy to burn someone to keep the heat off him and his group. I need an hour or two later to meet Angie, my sister, who's flying into Manchester Airport at lunchtime, we need to talk about mum's funeral and what she might have wanted. I'm hoping mum let Angie know because she never mentioned anything like that to me.'

'Take as much time as you need Steve. Did Sammy get in touch?'

'He did, he's probably working on her as we speak. I feel really detached from the situation with mum at the moment. Feels strange. I'll keep you updated,' Steve replied and left his bosses office.

***

'Okay team, again thanks for all being here nice and early. We've had a breakthrough in locating Paul Worrall,' said Steve. That made everyone in the room sit up and take notice. 'I might be actually guilty of using the word locating, I might be bigging up what actually happened.'

'You've definitely got everyone hooked up now Guv, don't keep us hanging,' said John.

'Okay John, didn't the nuns at your school ever tell you that patience is a virtue? Replied Steve, 'Last night while I was relaxing after a long hard day, like everyone else here, I'm guessing, I received a text message from, supposedly, Paul Worrall. I've got to tell you I have no reason to doubt that the man who sent it was Paul Worrall. This in itself poses many more questions than it answers.'

'You can say that again, why would he get in touch with you? What did he have to say?'

'Basically, without giving you the message verbatim, because it's no longer in my possession, it said that he knew I was trying to get hold of him for questioning regarding his mother's and brother's murders. He stated that a face-to-face meeting was out of the question, how he hadn't been in the UK for the last 3 years and how we'd never find him and how he wasn't the killer. He was obviously trying to mess with my head, which he achieved, and showing how he had all the power in our relationship and we had none.'

'Cheeky sod,' said Jude, 'What happened then?'

'Well Jude, I decided to take a screenshot for evidence and proof of what had happened in case he got it deleted. I didn't even know if he could actually do that. Believe me, he can and he did. He wiped out the message and all my screenshots too. He didn't need to do that; it was a relatively simple message. I think he just wanted to flex his muscles, show us what he could do.

The phone is currently with our techies at present. He did say if we wanted to ask him any questions then I should send an email to myself and he'd pick it up later. It's that easy for him, or so he likes to think. When I get my phone back it will be a completely clean phone except the text message app and software needed to run it. The only thing of interest will be a list of questions. Who knows, if he wants to, he might even give us a sacrificial lamb to get us off his back.'

'Why would he get in touch with us though? Asked Scott, 'I just don't get it, surely he's taking a big risk, he has no reason to, guilty or innocent.'

'That's a good question Scott, my thoughts are that he's a complete control freak and he needed to gain some sort of control. Let's face it, he's a cybercrime lord, it's his job to be a control freak. It will be very interesting to see how he answers the questions. I'll be out for a couple of hours this afternoon on personal matters so Jude, can you lead the team on the intel we're still looking for. John, can you see if you can get any information on Mark Green at the NCA. See if there's anything that suggests a possible leak. Paul Worrall has got my information from someone and it's a big coincidence that we were at the NCA only a few hours earlier. Shake the tree on him, see what falls out.'

'I thought he was a bit odd to be honest,' said John, 'and the fact that Paul Worrall has made contact with us doesn't make much sense to me.'

'It doesn't make a great deal of sense to me either.' Replied Steve, 'His only crime might be as a cybercrime mastermind, still a substantial crime, but nobody died. Whichever way you look at it the communication was unexpected and very unusual. It caught me off guard and in effect didn't tell us much about him that we couldn't have worked out for ourselves. It's contact though, and I'll take it and hope we get more like it. Okay everyone, keep me updated when you get anything you think might be pertinent. I'm going to come up with a list of questions that he may or may not answer.

Steve went into his office to come up with a list. He'd never had to interview a suspect via email but there's a first time for everything. If he was interviewing him face-to-face, he'd be able to read his body language and over the years he'd learned an awful lot about how to spot a lie looking at facial expressions and facial tics. The eyes could tell you a lot about the man or woman in front of you.

It felt like a waste of time when he'd been thinking of questions, if he asked where he was on the day of the murders, he'd be unlikely to be honest as he didn't even want them to know which continent he was in on the day of the murders, never mind which country. He wasn't going to admit to anything which meant he wasn't completely innocent. If he said he was in Mexico in a bar with a load of mates who could give him a solid gold alibi that would give the NCA a lead and he wasn't going to do that.

Even so, to not at least communicate would be wrong. He might give something away, he might even, with his cyber talents, be able to find the murderer from wherever he is in the world. The police can't just hack into someone's computer to find clues to lead them to a killer. If only, thought Steve but seeing as how it's a criminal offence he could be charged with cybercrime for doing it. There are probably countries in the world where police committing a crime to catch a criminal is completely acceptable, if hidden well enough. In the UK don't even think about it.

He decided to stick with a line of questioning that wouldn't piss Paul off and make him clam up.

From : Steve Wicks
To : Steve Wicks
Subject : Message for Paul Worrall
Hello Paul,

Thank you for opening a line of conversation yesterday, I certainly need to understand better what is possible in the cyber world. I'll take advantage of the opportunity afforded me and hope that, if you are as you say, innocent, you will at least be as honest as you can be in pointing us in a direction to follow. I have

been trying to understand why you contacted me to tell me you were innocent when I would be in the same position I'm in now if you hadn't contacted me. My reasoning leads me to believe you contacted me, if you are in fact innocent, because you want me to catch the murderer and are willing to help me achieve that goal in memory of your mother and brother.
1. Am I correct in this assumption?
2. Do we have a leak in the GMP, NCA, my team?

These are the only 2 questions I have for now but I hope I can ask more if needs be following your answers.

DI Steve Wicks

Steve read the email 3 times before he was satisfied. He'd decided to think of this as an opportunity rather than it being someone playing games with him. He'd take whatever lead he could at the moment, from whatever source he could.

Tony brought Steve his mobile phone back having made the changes he'd requested just as he finished reading the email through for the third time.

'Thanks Tony, I owe you one,' said Steve.

'I'll hold you to that mate,' Tony replied before turning around and leaving.

Steve picked up the phone and wasted no time in typing the email just as he'd handwritten it. Before he overthought it, he pressed send and away it went. He picked up his police issue phone and took a photograph of the email he'd just sent. He wasn't going to get caught out using a screenshot like last time.

Chapter Sixteen

Dave Greenwood called Steve and asked him to come to his office.

'Hello Steve, take a seat,' said Dave, pointing to a chair. 'I've had Sammy's initial findings, he got them to me before he normally would, knowing it was an important one.'

'Good, what did he say?'

'Your mum fell down the stairs, she wasn't pushed or at least there was no sign of it. Looking at your mum's recent medical history he could see she had been having chemotherapy for blood cancer…leukaemia in particular, I was surprised you've never mentioned it before.'

'Wait…leukaemia, you're not as surprised as I am guv. This is the first I've heard of it. Leukaemia. I've never mentioned it because I never knew, so I couldn't mention it. Leukaemia!'

'Steve, this must be a big shock if this is the first you've heard of it.'

'Why would she not tell me…' replied Steve with a questioning look on his face.

'Maybe she thought she'd beat it without you needing to know, maybe she didn't want to bother you with it.'

'I'm at a bit of a loss guv if I'm being honest. This has really thrown me.'

'Sammy says the treatment can cause patients to feel extremely fatigued and brain fog. I've heard of chemo brain before. Sammy says the fatigue and brain fog could have played a big part in her missing her footing at the top of the stairs causing her fall.'

'She could have come to live with me, if she'd told me. I'm all on one level, no stairs to fall down.'

'You know what mums are like Steve, always putting their offspring first, never wanting to be a nuisance. She was a healthy independent woman until she found out about the leukaemia; she probably valued her independence above her safety.'

'Well it didn't work out too well for her did it. Angie, my sister is landing at Manchester airport in an hour. She's in for a shock too.' Steve could feel the pressure growing, it could be anger at his mother for not saying anything, equally it could be sadness for the same reason. He needed to get some fresh air before his safety valve blew.

'Guv, I'll have to get some fresh air, go for a walk, gather my thoughts and try to make some sense of all I've just heard.'

'Of course Steve, take the rest of the day. If you need anything just let me know. Steve, don't feel bad about this, your mum in her mind thought she was doing the right thing. She had her reasons and you may never know or understand what those reasons were. Just try to respect the fact that she did what she did, and what in her mind, came from a good place.'

With that Steve nodded at his DCI and left his office without speaking further. It was only really now that Steve's mum's death was registering. He had thought he could ride it out and stay focused on the job at hand in finding a double murderer. He now knew that finding a murderer came a far second to the fact that his mum had died trying to keep her leukaemia a secret from him and, in his mind, had paid the ultimate price for it.

Steve had always prided himself on being level headed. It allowed him to function in the pressure cooker that life in his line of work could be. He was now beginning to think he was no longer as self-assured as he had been only an hour ago. Priority number one was to try to clear his head, meet Angie at his mum's place and explain what had been said about their mother's fall and what had caused it.

***

Steve unlocked the front door to his mother's house and found it very strange walking into an empty house. His mother's absence before this point felt unreal, now it was so real it felt painful. He would have to get used to the fact that he'd seen his mother alive for the last time. A few minutes later Angie pulled up and got out of her hire car.

'Hi Angie, good flight?' asked Steve.

'Uneventful, always a good thing in my mind. How are you? We've not really had a chance to talk since mum's fall.'

'I'll put the kettle on and make us a pot of tea. I've bought you some milk, bread, enough for a couple of days so we can at least have a brew. I feel like I could drink something stronger but mum wasn't much of a drinker. She's got a bottle of sherry but I think she bought it one Christmas when I was about three years old.'

'Sounds ominous…'

'Come into the kitchen, we'll carry on while I put the kettle on,' said Steve. 'Angie, did you know mum was having chemotherapy for leukaemia?'

'Leukaemia, no definitely not, it's not the sort of thing I'd forget. I knew nothing about this. If she'd told me in confidence I would have told you anyway. It's not something I could keep from you.'

'I know this might sound petty but I'm glad she kept it from both of us, not just me.'

'So mum had leukaemia and was having chemotherapy. She kept it all to herself but leukaemia didn't kill her, she fell downstairs or am I missing something here?'

'No, you're right, she fell down stairs, wasn't pushed as far as the post mortem can tell us. Apparently, chemotherapy can cause major fatigue and confusion. The thinking is that she was tired, confused at the top of the stairs, maybe turned around because she'd forgotten something, missed her footing and fell downstairs. The fall caused a brain bleed. She never really regained consciousness. She should have had a bed moved downstairs; she could have lived down here no problem.'

'Mum was a bit of a maverick Steve; she had some strong values. The last thing she would have wanted was to cause us any worry. She was old school don't forget. If she had lived downstairs during the chemotherapy that would have just caused us to question why. You know as well as I do, she would have seen cancer as a blip in life's journey for her to get over and move on from.'

'You're right of course,' replied Steve, 'it doesn't make it any easier that I lived less than a mile away from here and didn't pick up that anything was wrong from our conversations or seeing her when I visited. Some detective I am. It's no wonder this latest case is proving so difficult to get a break on.'

'Paul Worrall is a slippery bugger, clever beyond his upbringing and has a top team behind him and contacts hiding in plain sight across Europe,' said Angie.

'Angie, I've never mentioned Paul Worrall to you before, how come you know he's a person of interest to us regarding a double murder?'

'Confession time Steve, I work for the British government security services, seconded to Europol's cyber-crime unit. We believe that Paul Worrall is planning to destabilise the government via a blitz cyber-attack. He's been eluding my team for the past 14 months.'

Steve stood there looking at his sister words were a jumble in his head and he couldn't quite decide which to use first.

'I've wanted to know what you do for a while. MI5, MI6?'

'Steve, I've told you too much already and I've only told you because you're now my next of kin, you are the only person outside the department who knows this. It's not an MI department you will have ever heard of and you'll never get to know that, even when I die. I know you can keep a secret and if I tell you my life is at stake if this ever gets into the knowledge of more than a handful of people, you'll understand why it must not be told to anyone…not even Jude.'

'That's a lot to take in Angie, but why do you mention Jude? I take it you're talking about my detective sergeant. I don't know any other Jude.'

'That's right Steve, and I'm not being flippant, just wanting to show you that secrets can easily get out. If your life depended on keeping that a secret, you'd now be dead. So secret means absolutely no paper trail, nothing verbal, definitely nothing electronic. It's in your head now because I wanted it to be there. In there it stays. Agreed?'

'Agreed,' replied Steve, 'and I'm not even going to ask about how you know about Jude. Are you hungry? I know I've not eaten all day and there's a new Turkish restaurant opened in town. We could raise a few glasses to mum's memory. I don't think there's anything else you can tell me now that's going to surprise me.'

'In that case then why don't you invite Jude along too, get all the awkward introductions out of the way. Don't worry Steve your secret is safe with me… Agreed.'

'Agreed,' replied Steve chuckling to himself.

***

The following morning Steve was having his fourth cup of coffee and trying to get over the banging in his head from the previous night's drinking. He'd really enjoyed the night and it solidified in both himself and Jude that time was coming closer when they would put their heads above the parapet and tell their bosses about their relationship, frowned upon or not.

'Steve, I've just heard from the probation services regarding Simon Worrall, he was due to see his probation officer this morning but hasn't shown up. He's not answering his phone. He's been a good attender as far as his probation officer is concerned. He had a note in the file saying that he's on our radar so they've rung us to let us know, said John.'

'Have uniform been round to see if he's overslept?' Steve replied.

'Not yet guv, a big job's broken out and it's taking priority at the minute.'

'Okay, get yourself round there, take Scott with you see if you can raise him. If he's there, bring him in, if not get uniform to keep an eye out for him...when they've got someone available.'

'Okay guv, will do.'

***

John and Scott pulled up outside Simon's place and could see his curtains were still shut and the chances were that he'd overslept.

'Lazy bastard has one meeting to go to every week and he can't even drag himself out of bed for it,' said Scott.

'Let's try to wake him up Scott, useless sod,' replied John, 'no job, no prospects, no reason to get up. It comes to something when he won't even get up for his probation officer. They won't stand for that too many times before he's said to have broken his probation conditions and end up back inside.'

'From what I've seen of him so far, he's just a sad little man with a big chip on his shoulder, who feels like the whole world is against him. He'll be well pissed off when we wake him up. I'm looking forward to this to be honest.'

John rang the bell and waited for a response, after a short wait he put his finger on the bell and kept it there for 10 seconds. Still no response. 'If he's in there he doesn't want to come to the door.'

'Is there a case for making a forcible entry do you think?'

'Well let's have a look at it,' replied John, 'the boss wants him brought in, his living room and bedroom curtains are closed, he's not responding to the phone, he's not responding to the doorbell which we've pressed repeatedly, he's missed a scheduled meeting with the probation services which is unlike him, he lives alone and has already admitted to us that he has very few friends to check on his welfare.'

'I think that gives us good reason to gain entry on a concern for health basis, what do you think?' Asked Scott.

'Something isn't right, I'll get a locksmith on it, I don't want to break his door down, if he's only asleep. Uniforms are probably too busy to use the big red key on his door anyway.'

'Can I have a go at it first?' asked Scott. 'I've done a lock picking course. All above board and I've been waiting for an opportunity like this. Don't look at me like that John, nobody needs to know we were here if I can get in quickly and it does look like an easy lock to pick.'

'A man of hidden talents, knock yourself out Scott,' said John, grinning at the young DC.

They were walking through the door into the hallway 30 seconds later. 'Don't tell the guv though, as far as anyone else is concerned the door was unlatched, when we tried it, we just had to walk in.'

'Simon, are you in here?'

No response.

'Simon, we're coming in, fair warning.'

No response.

'Okay Scott, gloves on and we'll have a look round. I'll take this room; you take the next.'

'John, you had better come in here, I know why he's not been answering the door.'

Scott was stood at the door which opened onto a bedroom. John joined him there and looked in at Simon hanging by his neck from a hook in the ceiling which had obviously been placed there specifically for this purpose.

'That'll do it.' Said John.

'I think it's fair to say that we're too late and judging by the colour of his face a few hours too late.'

'Hanging by a short rope, hardly any drop, not a nice way to die. God knows how long it will have taken for him to die. Why wouldn't he just take an overdose, go to sleep and just not wake up.' Said Simon.

'Who knows what's going through a man's head when he gets to that point. Maybe though it wasn't suicide. We need to get a forensics team in, it might be murder number three.'

'That's one unfortunate family, must be cursed, two murders, maybe three. They must have really pissed off some people they really shouldn't have.'

John got his mobile phone out and rang Steve. 'Guv, we can forget bringing Simon Worrall in, we've just found him hanging from his bedroom ceiling.'

'Suicide do you think John?'

'At first look I'd say yes but given what's happened to his mother and brother I wouldn't bet my house on it…'

'I'll get a forensic team and pathologist mobilised from this end then I'll come over. Has he left a note at all saying why he did it?' asked Steve.

'We haven't been into the bedroom, don't want to contaminate a possible crime scene, but from what I've heard from him so far he's got nobody to leave a note for.'

'Yes, I think you're right with that one. I'll be over there soon.'

Steve made a couple of phone calls then went in search of Jude to let her know what had happened to Simon Worrall.

'I've been concentrating on the relatives, friends and relationships of the four people put away with David Worrall's help. I've got a few things worth following up on, I'll let you know how I get on tonight when I've got answers.' Said Jude after they had discussed the possible suicide of Simon.

Chapter Seventeen

Steve pulled up outside Simon Worrall's place to find John and Scott outside waiting for him.

'Hi John, Scott, how're we doing?'

'Well we're doing a lot better than Simon is.' Said John, we're waiting for the forensics and pathologist to turn up. We do have to let you know about something though guv, with it being a potential crime scene. It's how we gained entry to the flat.' Said John.

'Go on, tell me, I'm listening...'

'We had come up with reasonable grounds for gaining entry on danger to health grounds, I'm happy with that, and the uniforms are busy at the minute so we picked the lock instead of waiting for a locksmith to come out.'

'With concern for the residents health was it your fastest way of gaining entry?'

'Yes guv, 30 seconds and we were in.'

'And if the resident was in the middle of a serious medical episode, did it give you the extra time to possibly keep him alive while waiting for the paramedics to arrive?'

'Well yes guv, when you put it like that.'

'Okay then, I've got two things to say about it. Firstly, thanks for telling me. Secondly, be careful in future using that as a means of entry. You saved time in a concern for health call. We'll say no more about that.'

'Thanks guv.'

'Sammy is sending one of his minions. Thomas Corrie, probably because it's going to turn out to be a suicide. I think if he had a big hole in his head Sammy would be all over it. I've worked with him before, he's good. Show me the scene before he gets here, let's see him before he's cut down.'

'Scott, stay at the door and wait for Thomas Corrie to show up. I've brought some shoe covers and gloves,' said Steve.

Steve and John were careful to not move things they just ran their eyes over the room and quickly over the body hanging in front of them then got out of the bedroom and went back outside to join Scott.

'Looks like suicide to me,' said Steve, 'He's not a small guy, it would take 2 guys to overpower him and get him into position to hang him. If it's that much of a problem why not stick a knife through his chest and have done with it. There was no sign of a struggle within the room, his arms and legs weren't tied and I'd hazard a guess that there are no self-defence wounds from a struggle. If it's the same killer who killed his mother and brother it's a completely different MO. It's unlikely that we've got two different killers for 3 murders in the same family, all within the space of a few weeks.'

'He didn't take an easy way out by hanging himself with a short drop.' Said John.

'My money is on a suicide but let's hold our judgement until we get the report. One thing we can say, though, is that if Simon did kill his mum and brother, we're going to have to prove it posthumously. I'm going to get back to the station and leave you two here to deal with this. By the way Scott, good job with the door...' Steve winked and turned to leave.

'We'll see you later with any initial findings.' replied John with a grin on his face.

'How did he know it was me?' whispered Scott.

'Because I've been part of his team for four years and I've not once suggested picking a lock. Don't worry, if he wasn't alright with it, you'd be fully aware of that fact by now and my arse would be in a sling too being the senior office at the scene.'

***

Steve met Angie in the town centre on his way back to the station for a coffee and a bite to eat. Now that mum's body had been released Angie was going to visit a funeral director and give them the go ahead to pick up the body and get things arranged. They had almost finished eating when they got talking about what they were actually there for.

'We'll have to make a decision about the funeral service,' said Angie, 'mum wasn't a very religious person and she had mentioned a few years ago about not wanting a lot of fuss making.'

'I hadn't really thought about it much to be honest with you. One thing I can tell you though from experience is that no matter how many times you think you'll visit a grave it soon becomes less and less and life gets in the way.' Said Steve, 'Funny that, life gets in the way of death…I've just seen Simon Worrall, brother of Paul hanging from his bedroom ceiling. Life didn't get in the way of his death. I really need to take some flowers for Kim and Mia. It's a guilt I often carry with me and it's still a difficult task even now after 5 years, it still upsets me when I visit them.'

'I know it's not easy Steve, even after 5 years. Why don't we cremate mum and sprinkle her ashes in places that she liked to visit. I could carry part of her around with me in a necklace. That would make me happy.'

'I agree, I think mum would be happy with a small service at the crematorium. Simple, no fuss, it's what she would have wanted. I've started to think that as she was dying anyway with leukaemia and she really wouldn't have wanted to have a lingering death in a hospice, hospital or even at home. It's actually a blessing of sorts.'

'I found mum's will last night when I got back. No surprises there, basically she wants us to sell the house and car then split it between the two of us. I'll visit a solicitor after the funeral director and let them handle it all. We're both too busy to be involved in anything like that. I'll give them your name and number as main contact if that's okay. It's just easier with you living in Wigan.'

'Of course, that sounds best.'

'Right, I'm seeing the funeral director in 15 minutes so I'll have to love you and leave you little brother. I'm seeing a friend tonight and I'm getting a morning flight tomorrow but I'll contact you tomorrow evening with all the details of arrangements I know thus far.'

'Okay big sis, thanks for flying over and helping, I really appreciate it.'

'I'll be back for the cremation, and hopefully then with a bit more time I'll see more of Jude. I think you've made a good choice there Steve, she's lovely and you're both suited to each other. Mum would have loved her.'

'Thanks Angie, that means more to me than you can imagine. Have a safe trip home, love you sis.'
'Love you too brother, take care of yourself.'
***

Steve got back into the incident room much later than he'd expected. He'd just needed to forget work for a few hours with what had happened to his mum. It had been the first time he and Angie had sat down and talked for what felt like far too many years. Probably not since Kim and Mia had died 5 years ago. It had felt good to introduce Jude to Angie and just be brother and sister catching up on things.

Jude had been told by Angie that she worked in a small obscure museum in the Hague and Jude was just happy that she wasn't a fellow police officer or it would all be work talk and sometimes you just needed to talk to someone who had more layers than either she or Steve had. Steve smiled at this, accusing Jude of describing him as being two dimensional. Jude had punched him in the arm and said she was just the same as Steve and she was more than happy to think of being with a copper, especially Steve. At least he understood the job and life of a copper and the work expectancies. Most of the relationships she'd had in her life failed because of the job.

'Hi John, you can't have been back long, any news for me from this morning?' asked Steve.

'Initial findings were just as you expected,' replied John, 'unless the PM shows any other findings it's definitely looking like he took his own life.'

'Any idea where Jude is? I need to talk to her, she said she might be onto something and was going to tell me when she next saw me after following it up. She's not answering her phone, it's going straight to answerphone.'

'I've not seen her since we've been back but as I said I've only been back about 20 minutes. I know she was looking into Dave Burns, the OCG member who was killed in prison by a full life termer.'

'Emma might know where she is, she's been in most of today I think.'

Turning towards Emma, who was deep in thought looking at her computer screen Steve asked if she knew where Jude was.

'I saw her about a couple of hours ago but I haven't seen her since, I've been looking at this screen most of the time, or looking in archives. Really in another world. Sorry guv.' Replied Emma.

'She'll have turned her phone off while questioning someone and not turned it back on.' Said John.

'That's probably it.'

Steve went to his office and tried Jude again. Straight to answerphone again.

'Jude, when you get this message ring me back. I'm back in the office.'

Steve went down to the techies in the basement to see if they'd seen Jude at all in the last two hours. The answer was a resounding no.

'If you see her, tell her to turn her phone on and come and find me, I need to see her as soon as she gets back to the station.'

'Will do,' came the reply.

Steve could feel the concern growing in his stomach. Jude turning her phone off was unusual. She would turn it on silent rather than turn it off when questioning anyone, or giving bad news. She'd never turn it off. She'd normally tell someone where she was going if she went out on a follow up. Steve hoped she'd just dropped her phone and broken it. He'd give her another fifteen minutes then call her again unless she turned up in the meantime.

'When Steve got back from the basement, he went to talk to Emma again. 'Emma, Jude was working on finding family and friends of Dave Burns. She told me she was following up on something. Did she say anything to you about it? I'm just having trouble locating her at the minute.' Said Steve, 'I've been with my sister having a coffee and lost track of time.'

'I've been in and out of the office a lot today. She must have left while I was out of the office. I've been here for the last two hours though and she's not been in for at least that long. The office has been really quiet. Do you want me to try and contact her?'

'No thanks, Emma, I've left a couple of messages she should get when she gets back on her phone. It's nothing to get concerned about, I'm sure.'

Steve went to his office and closed the door, got out his phone and hit last number redial. Answerphone again, after half an hour he walked into DCI Greenwood's office.

'Dave, have you got a minute?'

'Of course Steve, what's bothering you?' replied Dave.

'It's probably nothing but I can't locate Jude, I've been trying for an hour but her phone is switched off and I've been leaving messages asking her to get back to me and she hasn't been in the office for two hours before that. I'm probably overthinking things.'

'You're not overthinking things Steve and you're right to bring it to me. Any concerns you have need addressing.'

'This is not like Jude, I've known her for a long time, we worked together in Manchester before coming here. She's usually contactable.'

'Let's deal with it, she'll probably turn up but until she does, I'll put someone on it.'

'Can't me and my team work on it Dave?'

'I'll give you two hours but then I'm bringing someone who's not too close to it in. First thing is to get a message to all uniforms to keep eyes looking for her and her car…I take it her car isn't parked up in the car park.'

'That's right, I checked earlier, it's not there.'

'Okay, let me check CCTV for when she left. Then hospitals need checking, say a ten- mile radius to start with. Get someone round to her place, check she's not there, check there hasn't been a break-in. Get someone working on what her phone's position was when it went dead, you might need to get the providers help on that to get a triangulation on last signal. Keep trying to contact her. Do we know of any close relationships she's in? Two hours Steve, if she's not been in touch in that time, I'm getting someone else in. Consider her a missing person from this time until we find her.'

'Thanks Dave, I'll get my team onto it now.'

Steve got back to his team and gathered them round.

'Do you remember the kidnapping case we had about 18 months ago?' Said Steve. 'Lucy Connelly, taken from Mesnes park in the middle of the day without anyone being aware of what had happened.'

'I do guv, caught the guy, Sam Jacobs, if I remember correctly, bit of a loner.' Said John, Lucy was unharmed but very shaken up by the whole experience.'

'That's right John. We need to be thinking along the lines that we've got another missing person…but this time it's Jude…and in a couple of hours we're going to be taken off the case because we're too close to it to be objective.'

'Bollocks,' said Scott, 'if anything we should be the ones on this, we know her better than anyone here.'

'I totally agree Scott but we're chasing a killer. Jude might have been in an accident and she's not been found yet. She might walk in the front doors of the station in the next 5 minutes, we don't know.'

'Or she might have got close to the killer and that's why she's missing. Jude's kidnapping, if that's what it is, maybe part of the case we're working on.'

'You're right Scott, I'm going to see if the boss will put a couple of detectives working on it but through this team, not independently. If she's got too close the killer it makes sense, but let's hope it's a kidnapping and not another murder. Drop everything you're working on for now.' Steve said.

'John, Jude's car has gone from the station car park. Dave Greenwood is going to look at CCTV to see if she left alone and when she left. Get a message to all uniformed officers to keep a look out for her car, grey Ford Puma, you'll get the registration on the system. Get a head shot of Jude from file too, get it circulated. Make sure they know she's one of us and it's urgent. Then see if she's been picked up on ANPR since she left the car park.'

'Yes guv, I'm on it.' Replied John.

'Emma check hospitals to see if she's been admitted. Start within a 10-mile radius.'

'I'll start that now.' Emma replied.

'When you've done that, see if you can find out what Jude was working on before she went missing. You'll probably need the help of the tech team to get into her files.'

'Scott, try to get a location for when and where Jude's phone was switched off.' Said Steve.

'Police issue and personal guv?'

'Yes Scott, they've both been switched off and that's very unlike Jude, she never turns her phones off.'

'I'll go round to where she lives to see if anything can tell me if she's been back there and look for signs of an abduction. I'll be back within the hour. If she turns up call me, if there's any news call me. This is everyone's priority number one. Let's assume she's been kidnapped and it's to do with the murders we're working on. The murderer has killed two people already, I don't want Jude to be number three. Shake the bloody tree hard this time.' With that Steve reached for his jacket and car keys and was out of the doors before they could say anything.

'Okay Emma, Scott 110 percent on this, let's get Steve some answers before he comes back.' John said, 'for the next couple of hours at least.

Steve first went to Jude's place; she had a rented a house in Shevington and knew she kept a spare key in the garage. He'd need to get his own key when this was all over. They would usually stay at Steve's if they were spending the night together and Jude had her own key to his place for the last month. The side door to the garage was always left unlocked but the key was well hidden and the garage almost empty of anything else except a few packing cases. She'd never even bothered putting the car away at night.

Steve had a quick look around the outside of the house. Jude's car was nowhere to be seen and there was no sign of any scuffle that may have happened with an abduction.

Inside he looked in every room trying to see if anything was out of place. He spent 10 minutes there but couldn't see anything out of the ordinary. She had spent last night with him and there was still post on the doormat which hadn't been picked up so he was fairly sure she hadn't been home. He decided to call in at his apartment to see if she'd called in there having forgotten something when she left that morning. She'd moved in quite a few clothes and toiletries, it just made things easier for them both when she stayed over. When this was resolved and she was back with him safe and well he'd make sure she moved in on a permanent basis. Angie had told him they were perfect for each other and what was happening now had made his mind up. It had taken him a long time for him to feel like he did about Jude after what happened to Kim and Mia. If she wasn't found safe and well, he didn't know if he'd be able to muster the strength to continue…his next thought was Paul Worrall…the only other person who knew about him and Jude, apart from Angie and maybe Tony from the tech team.

When he reached the car park for his apartment block, he could see Jude's car parked up. 'Thank God for that,' he thought, maybe she was just feeling unwell and had come back to his place for a lie down at lunchtime, because it was quicker than her going home. She'd then turned her phones off, fell asleep and was in his bed, safe and well.

On his way from the car park to his apartment he made a call to John to let him know he'd found Jude's car and that it was parked up outside his place. John just accepted it without questioning why she'd parked up there. 'Clever lad,' thought Steve.

He made his way up to his apartment, expecting to find Jude asleep on his bed like something out of Goldilocks and the three bears. He was surprised when there was no sign of her. Coffee cups were still where they'd left them that morning, the kettle was cold and the bed hadn't been laid on since he'd made it that morning. Everything said to him that she hadn't come inside since they left within 5 minutes of each other that morning. He was confused about why her car was parked up where she usually parked when staying over.

Making his way to his car reminded him of why he liked the location. The block was relatively new, in one of the better areas of Wigan, had only 6 apartments, described as an executive build, it was red brick and dressed stone. It didn't come cheap but he could afford it. Kim had been a lawyer and when she died the life and mortgage insurance had paid out a more than nice sum. As well as being high end the block was well back from the road which made it very private. If Jude had been abducted from here, he couldn't see any security cameras except doorbell cameras and the car park was around the side of the building entrance, all very private and isolated. It was good to live where everyone didn't know your business but at this time, he wished he'd lived in a much less private place, anywhere but here he thought to himself looking around. He got back in his BMW and pointed it towards Wigan town centre to report back to his team and Dave Greenwood.

Chapter Eighteen

Steve pulled up at the station and went directly to Dave Greenwood to report his findings.

'I went to Jude's house first,' said Steve, 'no sign of her or her car, no obvious signs of any abduction, no struggle, nothing unusual, nothing knocked over to suggest a struggle. I then went to my place…I'll tell you why in a minute, but when I got there Jude's car was parked up. I expected her to be inside, and now I need to admit something which, in fairness, I was going to mention soon anyway.' At that Dave looked at him with a raised eyebrow and said 'Go on.'

'Myself and Jude are in a relationship. It started out as companionship, both a little lonely, both in need of something more than work but too busy to find it outside of work. I know it's not great that we work together but it is what it is boss.'

'Is that it?' said Dave, 'you know it's not all that long ago that I wouldn't have been able to say this but it's not the police force's place to say who you can and can't have a relationship with. Can you imagine, in the woke society in which we now live that we can't at least let you have that relationship? The problems arise if and when a relationship goes South. Then we may need to step in and you both need to be aware of that. These things can cause many issues in the future but for now let's park that to one side and concentrate on finding Jude so you two can at least give this relationship the best chance at working for both of you. I take it she has a key to your place and her car being parked outside isn't unusual.'

'That's right boss, it's why I decided to call into mine on the way back. Did you find out when she left the station?'

'She left at 12.45pm so she's been out of touch for a good few hours now. I've told John, Scott and Emma already. She turned left out of the car park.'

'I don't even think she had been into my place, coffee cups exactly where they were left this morning, post on the doormat, which is delivered in the morning. Nothing to suggest she'd been inside. So she parked up at my place, didn't come indoors and disappeared leaving her car behind. Both phones switched off. She's either set off on a walk to clear her head and has fallen, knocking herself out where other people can't see her or she's got into another car with someone and they've driven off. I think we're dealing with an abduction and I think it's related to the murder case we've been working on.'

'I'm going to have to bring someone in on this after what you've just told me, you're too close to it, too emotionally involved to be impartial.'

'I agree I'm emotionally involved, but if she has been abducted, I'm thinking it must be to do with the murder case. She must have been getting too close to our murderer. If that's the case the abduction is part of my case. My money at this point is on Paul Worral, from a distance.'

'I'm going to have to take this one upstairs Steve and get advice on it. I think I might get away with bringing in a couple of detectives in to your team to work on the abduction, if that's what it is, and have them report to yourself and myself while you and your current team continue on the murders. I won't mention your relationship status with Jude at this point, as far as I'm concerned that's something you're going to tell me when Jude's found safe. Understood?'

'Understood boss.'

***

Steve made his way to his team hoping they had been able to find something, anything to point them in the right direction.

'So has anyone got anywhere regarding Jude? Maybe I should go first. No sign of Jude at her house in Shevington but her car was parked outside my place on Wigan Lane. No sign of Jude and just to let you know, but keep it strictly to yourself, me and Jude are in a relationship.'

'We've known about you and Jude for a few weeks now guv,' said Emma.

John and Scott looked at each other and both spoke at the same time, 'news to me.'

'Really, only me then, I thought it was obvious…must be a female intuition thing,' said Emma, 'you make a great couple boss.'

'Yeah, that'll be it,' said John looking at Steve as if to plead innocence.

'Okay, well thanks for keeping it to yourself Emma, until now. It's out now but only between us. It seems I'm much too close to Jude to work on her abduction, much too willing to take shortcuts and not follow the rules. Which is absolutely true. If it is an abduction though it's probably linked to the murder cases we're working at this time and Jude got too close to the truth. DCI Greenwood is trying to get me two extra people to work on Jude from this department under mine and DCI Greenwood's control. Two cases but potentially linked, it makes sense to keep them running from the same office. Anyone got anything to report, or questions to ask?' Asked Steve.

John spoke first. 'Any CCTV cameras covering the car park where you live?'

'Just doorbell cameras,' said Steve, 'It's too far back from the road and far too private to be honest. The car park had Jude's car and one other before I got there but the other car was David's who lives on the same floor as me, number 4, first floor. He's a writer and mostly works from home. So he may have seen someone drive in whose car he didn't recognise. Everyone else tends to be out Monday to Friday daytime working.'

'I don't think any of us is going home any time soon guv with Jude being out there somewhere,' said John, I'll give people another hour to get back home from work then I'll go and find out what the writer may have seen, check up on any cameras to see if there's anything been caught coming off the main road that doesn't usually park there. I don't think anyone will be assigned immediately, so we've got it covered until then.' Scott and Emma nodded their agreement.

'Good idea John, better it's not me questioning my neighbours, I really appreciate the commitment from the team. I'm still hoping she walks through the door and gives us a tale about how she fell over, banged her head and got confused but everything is okay now.'

'DCI Greenwood tells me she left the car park here at 12.45pm and turned left. Left or right it takes about 10 minutes to get to my place so if she went directly there, she would have got there at 12.55pm. Any later and she either got caught in traffic or went somewhere else first.'

'Last Signal from both her phones was 1.05pm around the Wigan Lane area, which all adds up with what we know so far,' said Scott, 'if she left here at 12.45pm she could have arranged to meet someone at 1.00pm. It all ties in so far for a timeline'

'See if you can get her tied into any ANPR cameras or CCTV cameras Scott. See if you can see her in the passenger seat of any vehicles after 1.00pm around Wigan Lane.'

'Emma, I'm taking it that there was no news from hospitals from what we know so far.'

'No news guv so far but I've made sure that if she does turn up in the next 24 hours, they'll let us know.'

'Good thinking Emma.'

'I've got nowhere getting into her files, Tony was due to come up but must be delayed. He knows it's about Jude having gone missing so he might be accessing her files remotely before he comes here.' Emma said.

'Okay, I'll chase up Tony, when he comes up I want you and me sat with him, I'm hoping it gives us some answers as to where she might be…'

Just as he was turning to chase him up Tony came through the door.

'Hello folks, I take it there's no news on Jude's whereabouts yet,' said Tony.

'Not so far Tony, we're hoping you might be able to give us some direction if you can tell us what she was looking at online this morning,' replied Steve. 'We're still hoping she hasn't been abducted and will walk through the door in the next few minutes but she left the station car park at 12.45pm and hasn't been contactable since shortly after. That's totally out of character for Jude.'

'Okay, Let's not waste any time getting into Jude's computer and take a look at what she's been working on earlier today,' Tony replied. 'Okay I'm in, the best I can do at this stage is let you know where abouts she's been as far as websites are concerned. Then I can have a look at keystrokes she's made, but that's going to take me longer and need some analysis. I'll have to do that from my computer in the basement. I'll have to run it through some specialist software but when it's done we'll get something that can tell us exactly where she's been on the websites and the inputs she made.'

'Thanks Tony, that's much appreciated and this is very time critical as you can imagine, for everyone here.'

'Okay, she's been on the Ancestry UK website, the UK deed poll office website. She was on these two the longest with a few others she also dipped into. I'll have a good look to see if I can come up with a timed replay of everything she did this morning but I'm going to have to run it throughout the night. It will be ready first thing when you come in tomorrow. If she came up with a name that caused her to jump in her car to go and investigate, you'll have it tomorrow morning Steve. I've also given you personal access to all Jude's files.'

'Cheers Tony,' Steve replied.

As Tony was leaving Dave Greenwood was walking into the office. 'Have we got anywhere yet Steve?'

'Tony says Jude was looking on the Ancestry UK site and the Deed Poll website. She had been looking at Dave Burns' family and friends and it appears she might have been following up on something when she left the station at 12.45pm.'

'Okay, I've got a DC and a DS temporarily coming into the team first thing tomorrow morning. That's the best I could do considering it's only been a matter of hours she's been missing. I've got the uniform section on high alert and we'll step everything up tomorrow morning if she doesn't make contact or turn up by the time we're back in tomorrow. We'll find her Steve.'

'Yes boss, I know we will. We might find our double murderer at the same time. Let's hope whoever that is, hasn't become a triple murderer.

'If anyone can find her Steve we can, and don't forget she's a canny lass, she'll be doing everything she can to survive,' said Dave, 'I would also say to the team that uniforms are searching around the Wigan Lane area. It's been dark for a couple of hours now but there will be a team with torches searching. Don't work into the night, it's better to get a sleep tonight and get clear heads together tomorrow when we'll hopefully know more.'

'She is a canny lass boss but we've got a few things we need to do before we leave for the day, we won't be here too long', replied Steve.

'Okay, Steve, I'll be here for another hour but I'm contactable at any time. My phone won't get switched off. If you get any news or need anything pushing through just contact me, any time.'

With that DCI Dave Greenwood went back to his office and Steve spoke to his team.

'The boss is right; there's not much we can do at this point until we know more tomorrow. Uniforms are doing a search but it's not going to be easy in the dark. John, I'll do a check if anyone has got any CCTV at my place.'

'Like you said guv, better if I do it, I'll do it on my way home, shouldn't take too long,' John replied.

'Okay John thanks, I've got a couple of things I need to do then I'll get off. Scott, Emma, you two get off home soon, Jude's going to need us on top form tomorrow. I'll be in my office if anyone needs me.'

When he got back to his office, he checked his personal emails for a reply to the one he left for Paul Worrall. It was sat there waiting for him.

To : Steve Wicks
From : Anonymous
Subject : Answers to your questions
DI Wicks,
My answers to your questions are-
1. Yes, I will help if I can, I want the murderers caught.

2. Is there a leak…no comment

<u>Anonymous</u>
So there was a leak, otherwise he would have said no, surely. It was obvious he wanted to protect his source and Steve could understand that. That's one to be looked at further when he has more time to investigate it later. For now finding Jude and the murderer were his priorities.

He decided to ask a question regarding Jude.
To : Steve Wicks

From : Steve Wicks
Subject : Jude Lawler – Message for Paul Worrall
Paul,
We believe DS Jude Lawler has been abducted whilst working on the murders of your mother and brother. Do you have any thoughts on this?
I also have to tell you that your brother Simon was found dead in his flat this morning. At this stage it looks like he committed suicide. I'm sorry to have to tell you this via an email but it's my only way of communication.
<u>DI Steve Wicks</u>

Steve then rang Angie.
'Hi Angie, I hope I've not interrupted anything but I need to talk.'
'What's happened Steve? Something has, I can hear it in your voice.'
'It's Jude, she's been missing since midday, her phones were both switched off at 5 past 1 and her car is parked up at my place. It looks like she never went inside.'
'Damn Steve, I'm sorry to hear that. Let me speak to someone in London and I'll get straight back to you.'
'Okay Angie, speak soon.'
That was Angie, he thought, no messing, no waffling on about what was happening. Instant understanding and no messing about. Plan already formed in her mind and ringing someone to run it by them. That's what he'd hoped anyway.
All he could do now is wait for Angie to get back to him. He didn't know how long that would be so he went to check that his team would be on their way home soon.
John had left already and was probably questioning people at Steve's apartment block about what had happened today and seeing if anyone from the neighbourhood had CCTV which would point them in a direction to follow. Scott and Emma were just putting their coats on ready to go home.
'See you early tomorrow guv,' Emma said 'We'll find out exactly what she was working on tomorrow and we'll get the bastard who's responsible.'

Just then his mobile phone started ringing and he could see it was Angie calling. He said goodbye to Emma and Scott and made his way back to his office to answer the phone.

Chapter Nineteen

Jude woke up and tried to open her eyes. That wasn't going to happen just yet she thought. She had her Sunday morning head on, the one that keeps on saying 5 more minutes. Then she remembered it wasn't Sunday morning but was struggling to remember much of anything else. She was confused and couldn't put together what had happened to bring her here, wherever here was.

She was lay down on a mattress in darkness, apart from the very poor light given off by a night light. She could faintly see that she was in a room, a small room with just a mattress to sleep on. No windows but her eyes were beginning to adjust to the faint light available. She decided to get up off the mattress to explore where she was, that was when she realised that she was chained around her ankle to a point on the floor, the metal floor. Looking around she realised that she was in a small shipping container. The floor size was approximately 8feet by 8feet. The chain was loose enough for her to stand up but when she did, she almost immediately fell back onto the mattress. She had become very dizzy, like all the blood had decided to visit her feet. She sat up slowly and put her head between her knees until she wasn't dizzy any longer.

She was wearing a grey tracksuit, many sizes too big, which she would never have chosen for herself, had she been given a choice. Her watch was gone along with her phones, bag, clothes and shoes. She had a pair of slipper socks on which she was grateful for, being in a metal room. She stood up, slowly this time. She could see a door at the far end of the container but couldn't get anywhere close to it because of the chain. If she was in a shipping container it had been modified, maybe for use as a workshop she guessed. There was a small heater on the far wall which was keeping the temperature at a level that was comfortable. It wasn't a room that she would ever describe as inviting, however. There was a chemical toilet which she could just reach and drag closer, for which she was very thankful. It wasn't ideal but at least it was a toilet none the less. There was also a 1 litre bottle of water, unopened, and a packet of sandwiches. She wasn't hungry yet but she had a raging thirst. She took the top off the bottle of water and took several large swigs from it, as if she hadn't had a drink for some time. She had no idea how long she'd been in the container and couldn't remember getting here or who it was that brought her here, her memory was letting her down, badly. She usually had a very good memory, it certainly helped in her line of work, it wasn't always an advantage though because there are some things she'll never forget because some things you just can't unsee.

Her police brain was starting to kick in but her recent memories were just out of reach at this time. She was beginning to think that she must have been drugged at some time to make her compliant, get her clothes changed and keep her like a prisoner in a cell. She could remember Steve and that brought a smile to her face, she knew the police would be putting in some effort looking for her.

Her stomach was now starting to tell her she needed to eat something. She ripped open the box of sandwiches, Marks and Spencer Roast Chicken Salad. At least her captor had good taste in sandwiches. Judging by her thirst and hunger she guessed she hadn't eaten in 12 or more hours. She couldn't tell if it was night or day. If her captor, or captors had been looking to confuse her they had clearly done a very job of that.

The small electric heater suddenly came on. She didn't know if it was on a timer or governed by the temperature in the container. She was thankful for the heat and thought it must be getting colder outside so she thought it might be evening. She didn't have a duvet for the mattress and she knew without the heater she would be freezing.

She couldn't hear anything except the heater. There was no traffic noise, no people speaking, no animal noises. She guessed she was somewhere remote, maybe in a farm building or in an empty factory unit. She started shouting for help but with nobody showing up after 5 minutes she gave up shouting and all she could hear again was the sound of the heater.

She was suddenly very tired again and had to lay down on the mattress before she fell down. Within a minute she was in a deep sleep again, 10 minutes after she had placed her head on the pillow the door opened and someone came in, wearing a gas mask they placed a blanket over her and replaced the sandwiches and water. She wouldn't be awake for a few hours yet, whoever was responsible for her kidnap had made sure of that.

***

Steve picked his phone up in his office.

'Hi Angie.'

'Hi Steve, I spoke to my boss in London and let him know what has happened to Jude. He's given me compassionate leave until this is resolved, or until Monday, whichever comes first. I do need to be back in the Hague on Monday to tie a few things together, so I'm booked on a flight to Schiphol airport on Sunday. I will be back for mum's funeral after I've set things up.'

'That's great Angie, we haven't heard anything as yet from any kidnapper, no ransom request. I'm going home soon, I'll put my walking gear on, get my torch out and have a walk round local to my place. I know I probably won't find anything but I can't do nothing, it's cold, it's dark and at this stage I just need to know she's alive. If she's been kidnapped at least she should be being kept alive somewhere warm and dry, but the longer it takes to find her the bigger the chance of us never finding her.'

'I agree, if she's out in this weather overnight it's not good, I'll come and help too. If you take your side of Wigan Lane, I'll take the opposite side. Agreed?'

'Agreed, said Steve, I'm going home now and I'll start shortly after that.'

'I'll be there in about half an hour if you see any signs of struggle in your area let me know and I'll come direct to you. I have to warn you Steve, we're probably not going to find her but we both know that it's of high importance to try. I'll see you at half past ten at your place.'

Steve already knew that in other people's view they were probably wasting their time but the last thing he was going to do was not try and while he had a breath in his body that would always be the same until she was found.

At 10.30pm Angie and Steve were sat in Steve's apartment with hot mugs of coffee, having failed to find anything that would point them in Jude's direction.

'If she's been abducted, I wish whoever had done it would let me know that she's safe,' said Steve.

'Unless they want a ransom to be paid, they would have no reason to get in touch though Steve, that would be just handing you clues to who they are and they won't want to do that. In my opinion you were right when you said that Jude had got too close to the killer and that killer has decided to take her out of the equation. Temporarily, I hope. The killer, if that's who it is, has managed to kidnap a Detective Sargeant and at this stage left no clues so whoever it is, they're working at a high level. They will know, however, unless they are really ignorant, that the police will be able to follow whatever Jude was doing to bring them to her notice and come to the same conclusion as Jude did.'

'Hopefully, early tomorrow will give us that information and when we have that we will probably have the name of the killer and the best way of getting Jude back alive.'

'As I said though little brother, it's not a massive leap for the killer to understand that too, unless they are from the lower end of the intellect quotient, and sadly I don't think that's the case. From what you've told me so far, the killer hasn't just walked into a house and killed the two people for fun. One of the dead gave up four people to the police, helping to put those four people behind bars. That's got revenge written all over it so there is a very big chance that those killings were well planned and played out just as they wanted them to be played out. Is the killer trying to distract you from completing the job of catching him or her, or, and you have to consider this Steve, is Jude the third victim and the killer has fled already?'

'I know this might not work out the way I want it to Angie but I'm just trying to stay positive amongst all what's going on. I have to believe that Jude is still alive,' said Steve, 'otherwise what's the point in going on? Life is difficult as it is with all the crap that goes on that needs to be policed. It's my job to do that policing and I can handle that, along with my team. If Jude is dead, I really don't think I could ever get past that. I lost Kim and Mia so I know it takes so much effort to feel anything like normal again. I threw myself into work, shut out the pain. It was probably the only way I could get myself back on track. A person should only have to go through that once in life if at all. Here I am looking at the possibility of going through it a second time. I could not go through that again.'

'I know Steve, let's hope you don't have to. The thing that's in our favour is that until we hear differently, she's still alive and until then it's that that drives us forward,' replied Angie, 'in my opinion she's definitely been taken. If she was meeting someone regarding some intelligence that she found during the investigation then it was probably someone she knew and was meeting them to rule them out once and for all. She didn't believe they were the killer, if she had she definitely would not have met them alone, she's too good a copper for that, been doing the job too long to do that.'

'you're right about that, I've known her a long time and she's a good copper.'

'If she knows them there's a good chance you know them too. She felt comfortable enough to meet them by herself and when I met her, she didn't give me the impression she's a risk taker. She has every reason to not take risks little brother, it's obvious that you two are so in love and if I know women like I do, she's not going to put that in jeopardy for anybody.'

'I know Angie, we really have to find her alive, in my world there really is no other option. A different outcome just can't exist.'

'Nor in my world,' said Angie, 'I'll sleep in your spare room tonight if that's ok. I have to go to the Manchester office first thing tomorrow but I'll keep in touch. If you need my help with anything I'm here for you. Anything I'm able to do I can do really well. Don't forget I'm ex-military with years in intelligence and field work... Don't forget that.'

'I won't forget. I'd better get to sleep if I can, I think it's going to be a busy day tomorrow, good night Angie'

'Good night, Steve, see you in the morning before you go into the station.'

***

Jude woke from a nightmare and when she opened her eyes to the weak light, she remembered she didn't need to dream a nightmare, she was already living out a nightmare. She still couldn't grasp from the depths of her memory how she had got to where she was or who... She just couldn't make the leap from where her mind was to where she needed it to be. It would surely come in time but time wasn't something she could be sure of having. She knew that at any time, someone could walk through the door and take her face off with a double barrel shotgun without her ever being aware of who it was holding the shotgun. She was still alive though and at this time that was all that mattered and the longer she stayed alive the better her chances were of staying that way.

Staying alive was key and at this time she had water to drink, food to eat and air to breathe. Everything she needed in the short term. Her abductor was giving it all to her. If only she could remember who that is.

***

At 7.00am Steve pulled into the station car park and backed into a space near to the building entrance. He wanted to be able to get away to wherever the day took him quickly. He switched off the engine and took a deep breath. Knowing what he wanted to happen today and getting that to happen probably lay in the hands of Tony and what happened in the next hour or two.

When he entered the investigation room, he was met by two detectives, a sergeant and a constable.

'Hello DI Wicks, I'm DS Paula Stevenson and this is DC Simon Hayes. We're here to help on the missing person case and seeing as how that person is one of our own, we're keen to get started sir.'

He took in the two detectives quickly. DS Stevenson was short and looked like she was about 8 stones wet through. He'd heard that in Paula Stevenson's case you shouldn't judge the book by the cover. A judo international at the last Olympics she could handle herself against any copper in the station unless they took her by surprise and even then, she was probably going to have most of them on the floor before they realised what the pain in their head was. DS Simon Hayes was a big lad, handy on a rugby field he was also very capable. DCI Greenwood had managed to get hold of two really good coppers in a short time. Steve also understood that if they hadn't found Jude by the end of the day, two coppers was probably going to turn into twenty.

'Glad to see you both nice and early, your reputations as good detectives are well known so I'm very happy. Today is going to be a massive day, as you no doubt know DS Jude Lawler went missing yesterday at midday and we've heard nothing from her since. Phones have been switched off since 5 past 1 yesterday afternoon. Any searches have been done in the dark so not ideal but nothing seen so far. Another team will be out in daylight today to see if there was anything they missed. You'll need to liaise with the search team during the day.' Said Steve, 'And sir is way too formal for me, Guv will do. Tony from the tech team is due in soon with the findings of what Jude was investigating yesterday morning on her computer. Hopefully that will give us a name or a strong direction to follow. When he's had time to look at the findings he's coming straight over so take those two desks on the right, and when Tony's here I need you two up front and centre. For now though get yourself a coffee and try to get up to speed with where we're up to.

'Okay guv, will do, I see John has just walked in, we started on the force at the same time, we know each other well, we'll liaise with him and get up to speed,' said Paula.

'Great, Paula, Simon good to have you both here and welcome to the team. I'm sure I don't need to tell you how important this case is, a lot of people will be looking over our shoulders with Jude being one of us. I really feel like it's going to break in the next hour so get ready to strap in tight because it might get hectic later.'

With that Steve went back to his office, logged into his computer and took a minute to get his head in the right place. At the moment he didn't have control over the kidnapping, he picked the phone up and got hold of Tony Hill.

'Hi Tony, where are we at with what Jude was specifically working on before she left the station at midday yesterday?' Asked Steve.

'Hi Steve, we're nearly there, give me half an hour and you'll be able to see it all played out on screen,' replied Tony.

'Good man Tony, we're all champing at the bit over here.'

'I hear you Steve, I'm not working on anything else, this has been given top priority by those who fly their offices at the dizzy heights you and me can only dream of.'

'Cheers mate, see you when you're ready.'

Steve decided to see Dave Greenwood and tell him he might want to be in the investigation room when Tony Hill gets there.

***

Jude woke up slowly again, she didn't know what drugs she'd been given but she felt like she'd been drained of all her energy. 'Probably easier for the kidnapper if I'm totally compliant,' Jude thought, 'Whoever it is doesn't want me anything other than pliable or asleep' She wondered what Steve was doing about her kidnapping. If she got out of this alive, she was going to claim her man and she didn't care who knew about it. The time was right for both of them. There was just the little matter of being kidnapped to overcome but she knew Steve and the team would be all over it. She had the feeling that whoever kidnapped her she'd known before the kidnapping. Something was niggling at the back of her mind, like she was getting closer to getting a memory back a little piece at a time. Or maybe she was overthinking it. She did trust her mind though. It was active seven days a week, fifty-two weeks a year.

She reached for a bottle of water and saw it was another fresh one alongside a couple of bacon and egg baps which she was ready for and quickly ate. She didn't know what day it was or what time it was but she was willing to bet the bacon and egg baps were for breakfast. This must be day two but she thought without outside light it could be day three or even day four. She had no idea how long she'd been asleep and was unaware of any interaction she may have had with her abductor. She was very hungry when she woke so she might have been asleep for twenty-four hours. She was sure the kidnapper was feeding gas into the container to knock her out allowing someone to enter the container and resupply food and water and empty the chemical toilet. She also woke under a blanket which she hadn't had previously. The kidnapper wasn't just playing at this, whoever it was had thought it through and at this stage were in complete control of the situation. Jude had not a clue who it was who was controlling her life.

Looking around she could see four bottles of water and a whole selection of sandwiches. She didn't think she'd be put to sleep for the rest of the day because the kidnapper had left food and drink that would last two days. Then she started overthinking her situation…What if only one person knows where I am and that person is involved in a car accident and dies… Who will find me? Will anyone find me? four bottles of water won't last forever.

'Don't think like that Jude,' she said to herself, 'you're not that person, you know nothing about the kidnapper, don't start thinking the worst, you're a logical person, stay positive.'

Eating the bacon and egg baps had made her tired again. 'Shit, they weren't sealed in a carton like the previous sandwiches had been, they were in a couple of white paper bags,' she thought to herself. As her eyelids got heavier and she tried to fight it the last thing she thought was nice tasting baps but drugged…you complete amateur. To be fair she'd never been in this situation before so she was winging it. She wouldn't make that mistake again she promised herself as her eyelids finally gave in to a heavy sleep.

Chapter Twenty

Tony Hill walked into the investigation room and felt all eyes upon him.

'Hi folks, I'll set up this laptop on this desk, you'll probably want to all watch this,' said Tony, 'it'll go through every key stroke Jude made yesterday while she was logged onto the system. It will bring up the pages she was on. We can pause it at any point but it shouldn't take too long as it gets rid of big pauses…so probably in about twenty minutes you'll know everything she was looking at yesterday morning. I'll set it up through the projector so we see it big enough for everyone to see. If you need me to pause it at any time, just ask.'

'Thanks Tony, sounds perfect.' Said Steve.

By the time he was set up and ready to go there were eight pairs of eyes eager for the show to begin. They had been watching the speeded up run through of Jude's key strokes and the screens she would have seen on the morning before. After about ten minutes Steve was beginning to think that it was going to be a dead end because they hadn't seen anything pertinent to her kidnapping. The screen then showed that Jude had gone onto governments deed poll office website. When Steve saw the name Jude had typed in, he spoke up to the rest of the room,

'Can you pause it there please Tony.'

'No problem.' Replied Tony.

'That must be a mistake, what do you think Dave?'

DCI Greenwood was looking a little perplexed too, 'maybe we need to watch some more, see what comes of it.'

The name she'd typed in was Samuel David Lomas and what popped up next was a number to contact.

'Date of birth 1st June 1970, looks to be in the right ball park, he'd be early to mid-fifties now.' Said Steve.

Scott was looking confused, 'Can you fill me in who this bloke is guv, I've not got a clue.'

Tony paused the screen.

'Sorry Scott, you've possibly never met him but I'm guessing you've seen his signature on pathology reports before now.' Replied Steve

'You're talking about Dr Sammy guv?'

'That's right Scott, Dr Sammy, that's why I'm saying it must be a mistake, I'm going to ring the deed poll office, see if they can throw some light on it. Start the screen again, see where she went next.'

Steve made his way to the back of the room and phoned the number he'd written down off the screen.

'Hello, this is DI Steve wicks with the Greater Manchester police force ringing from the Wigan Station. One of my colleagues will have been in touch yesterday following up on an enquiry to do with a possible murder suspect who may have changed their name in the past. Can you put me in touch with someone who she may have spoken to please.'

'Of course, please hold the line.'

After about twenty seconds, which felt like forever to Steve, a voice came on the line.

'Hello, DI Wicks, this is John Turner, I'm usually the person who fields all the enquiries from the police. How can I help you?'

'Hello John, it sounds like I'm speaking to the right person. A colleague of mine, DS Jude Lawler, will have rung your office yesterday, late morning, regarding a possible suspect in a murder case we're currently working on.'

'I remember her, charming lady, just let me get the notes up on my screen…Yes, she was asking me if a man called Samuel David Lomas had previously changed his name.'

'That's correct, Samuel David Lomas, date of birth 1st June 1970. DS Lawler is unavailable at the moment for me to ask, can you tell me what you told her yesterday?' Asked Steve.

'Of course, I've got the details of the conversation up on my screen. This is a person who had a name change in 1973, his mother did all the paperwork as the young lad would have been just under three years old at the time. The name change was to give him his step father's surname. His name prior to the change was Samuel David Burns.'

'And the mother's name, would that be Sarah by any chance?'

'Yes, indeed it was.'

'John you've been a big help, thank you.'

'Always happy to help.' Replied John.

When Steve had put the phone down, he returned to his colleagues and asked Tony Hill to pause the screen.

'Okay, I never thought I'd be saying this to anyone but Sammy…Dr Samuel David Lomas, to give him his full name has now become our number one suspect in a double murder case and hopefully just the kidnapping of our colleague Jude. If only we hadn't been so busy yesterday and I hadn't decided to meet with my sister to make decisions about my mother's funeral Jude may not be missing now.'

Dave Greenwood then spoke up to put Steve right on that. 'It's the fault of nobody in this room that Jude is missing. I'm really struggling to think that Sammy, a man I would call a friend, is responsible, and as of yet we don't know for sure that it is him. Jude didn't feel the need to say anything yesterday and I'd be willing to bet my house on the fact that she met him just to rule him out. He's one of the solid good guys in the world, a prince amongst men.'

'I agree boss,' replied Steve, 'but I haven't finished yet. Sammy's name, up until the age of nearly three, was Samuel David Burns, born on 1st June 1970 and his mother's name, who made the application to the deed poll office was Sarah Lomas. David Burns, who Dave Worrall helped us bang up, along with Derek Wilson, Bill Davis and Jonny Stevens, was killed by a whole life term prisoner inside Manchester prison. I'm betting he was related to Sammy. The same Sammy who we know as a pathologist and whose mother's name happens to also be Sarah.'

'That's a lot of fingers suddenly pointing towards Sammy.' Replied Dave Greenwood.

'Means, motive and opportunity,' replied Steve. Means, there isn't much Sammy doesn't know about how to kill someone, he's seen more killings than most people in his time as a pathologist. He's spent years becoming qualified for it. Motive, Dave Worrall played a key part in putting Dave Burns away, and Dave Worrall is one of our murder victims. Opportunity, he might have been planning this for years, keeping a regular eye on Karen Worrall's place on the off chance of her son turning up for a visit.'

'Okay, Steve, you've convinced me. Find Sammy we find Jude or find Jude we find Sammy. I need to take this upstairs now, get a much bigger team on it. Let's be under no illusions, Jude is looking like another victim of our killer. There is nothing we can do about the two that are already dead but we can find Jude, hopefully safe and well.'

DCI Greenwood left the room to report to the 'Gods' of policing in Wigan to confirm that it was nearly 100% sure that Jude had been kidnapped or worse by practically one of their own. More man power was his wish, especially backup from uniform, after all, Jude had very likely been abducted by their number one murder suspect. He was still trying to get his head around the fact that Sammy was the killer. He had said that, in the past, in his time as a member of the Greater Manchester Police Force there was nothing that could surprise him anymore. He knew now that was no longer true.

Making his way back to his office he had the unenviable task of getting in touch with Jude's next of kin to confirm that Jude's plight was definitely being treated as a kidnapping and that all efforts were being made to get her back safe and well.

***

'Okay team, quick instructions before me and John head off to the morgue to see Sammy. I'm guessing he won't be there but it might give us some leads. Then we'll visit his mother,' said Steve. 'Scott and Emma, I need you to find out what properties Sammy has in his portfolio. He has a number of rental properties in and around Wigan, look for addresses that Samuel David Lomas and Samuel David Burns DOB 1st July 1970 owns. Start at the land registry then look at local companies that manage lease properties on behalf of owners, he's likely to have them all with a single company, probably an estate agent. Find out if any are empty at the minute. Paula and Simon, you head off and check out his home address, you'll get it off the system. I'm not expecting him to be there, too obvious, but look to see if his car is parked up nearby or in his garage. He drives a Jaguar F-Pace, top of the range, black, as his daily drive but I know he also has several classic cars. Check his garage, it's massive, he can fit at least 6 cars in there. Remember, if you have reason to believe someone's life is in danger you can enter without a warrant. Understood?'

'Understood guv,' Paula replied.

'Good. Scott, we need a list of all the vehicles he owns, again look at Samuel David Lomas and Samuel David Burns. Make, model, colour, registration…get onto DVLA. When you have that list get it out to uniform and let's try to find where they are. When we know what properties Sammy owns start looking at his relatives and properties that they own. I know he liked to go fishing in Scotland, see if he has any properties that he could use as a holiday getaway.'

'Paula, Simon, when you've been to Sammy's house let me know what you find then get back here, I need you to look at his finances. What has he been spending in the last month as a starting point, see if there are any clues jumping out at you. Anything that points us towards Jude. Okay everyone, I don't need to tell you how important this is, shake the tree as hard as you can…for Jude.'

Five people said 'yes guv,' in unison. Steve and John were out of the office and in Steve's car within thirty seconds. The sense of urgency was palpable.

'Okay John, drive to the mortuary, let's see if life could be that easy…' said Steve, knowing it could never be so easy with someone like Sammy. He realised in that moment that if Sammy was the killer, he'd performed all the autopsies of the people he'd killed and he'd also done the autopsy after his mother died, saying it was an accident. Steve took his phone out of his jacket pocket and rang Angie first then Dave Greenwood.

Angie agreed that the sensible thing to do would be to get their mother's autopsy looked at again to see if anything could be seen that Sammy 'missed' either intentionally or unintentionally. Dave Greenwood would put everything in motion regarding his mother's autopsy. It would be difficult to see if she had been pushed or tripped but if she had any drugs in her system that shouldn't be there and Sammy didn't report on it really could point the finger at Sammy being a serial killer.

John parked out of sight of the mortuary. He didn't want to give Sammy the heads up on their arrival, even though windows were at a premium in the mortuary building, apart from in the attached offices. Neither Steve or John was expecting Sammy to be there, his black Jaguar was nowhere to be seen. They needed to find out what he had told the people he worked with as to his sudden absence from work if he wasn't there.

   Steve pressed the buzzer to the entrance door and looked up towards the CCTV camera so they could see who it was making an unannounced visit. The door was unlocked and the pair walked in.

   'Hello,' said Steve to the lady who had buzzed them in. 'It's Julie, isn't it? I saw you recently when Sammy completed an autopsy as part of his GMP duties.'

   'Yes, I remember, it's DI Wicks, isn't it?' she replied.

   'That's correct Julie, we need to speak to Sammy urgently if you could get him for us, please.'

   'Sammy isn't here, unfortunately, he booked a last-minute short break, he's not expected back until next Monday.'

   'Don't get your hopes up for Monday,' thought Steve.

   'That is unfortunate,' he said, 'did he say where he was going by any chance? Probably Scotland if I know Sammy, he loves to get some fishing in if he can, no matter what the weather is.'

   'I don't know to be honest. I wasn't here when he announced it but let me get hold of Helen, she might know.' Julie picked up her phone and got through to Helen but she couldn't say either. 'Sorry, she doesn't know,' said Julie, 'he was in such a rush yesterday apparently. Very unlike Sammy, he can usually talk the hind legs off a donkey, given 5 minutes free time.'

   'That's Sammy alright. Okay Julie, no problem, I'll try to get hold of him on his mobile.'

   'I've tried already this morning,' said Julie, 'I think wherever he is the signal isn't very good, so you might be right, if he's fishing in Scotland the signal might not have very good coverage.'

   'Thanks for your time Julie, I'll keep trying,' said Steve.

   'If he sees I've been trying to get hold of him he'd usually ring back when he has a missed call. If he does, I'll tell him you're trying to get hold of him.'

   'Thanks Julie, that would be perfect, if you could tell him I need to speak to him on an urgent matter I'd be very grateful.'

   Steve and John made their way back to the car.

'I didn't expect he was going to be there…unless we'd got this whole thing wrong and I'm more convinced now that Sammy is our man. It makes so much sense, we were floundering with the murders because even though Sammy was there in plain sight at the murder scenes it has really taken everybody by surprise, Jude too by the look of things. Sometimes plain sight is the best place to be,' said Steve.

'That makes sense,' replied John.

Once they were back in the car Steve rang Dave Greenwood to see about a blanket warrant to cover all properties owned or leased by Sammy and let him know, as expected, Sammy wasn't in work and was not contactable. They were heading back to the station and they expected to be there in 5 minutes.

'We need someone with special skills I think, warrants take time and we haven't got time to waste.'

John looked across at his boss…'Scott, and his lock breaking skills. Skills we only recently discovered?' asked John.

'Exactly. Let's use those skills if we need to. If we're waiting on a warrant and we need to get in somewhere we can at least be as covert as possible. I'll do anything I need to find Jude, and like the boss said, find Sammy we'll find Jude.'

'Where to next guv? Asked John.

'Back to touch base and see where everyone is up to. Re-evaluate and reform our thoughts.'

'We'll be there in 5 minutes guv.'

Steve and John, jumped out of the car and made their way up to see who was in from the team and catch up on where everyone was up to.

'Scott, you're coming with us after this catch up…bring your tools along, just in case.'

'Yes guv, will do,' said Scott with a smile on his face, happy to be helping with his own speciality.

'Emma, have you got any addresses for us to look at yet?'

'Yes guv, it appears that Sammy has 4 rental properties in the area and he also owns a place in the Lake District, Grasmere. I'm guessing a holiday place but we couldn't find it on any holiday leasing company's books. He's only had it for 3 months so might not have even used it yet.'

'Emma, Scott that's great work, keep digging Emma. That's 6 properties so far. I'll get in touch with the Cumbria Police Force and let them know we'll be on their patch. John, how do you fancy a trip to Grasmere?'

'You know me guv, I'll go to the Lakes at any time. I'll get out of this suit, put some warm clothes on so I blend in and a change of clothes just in case I need to stay over. Emma, write the address down and I'll be on my way up there.'

'Good man John, let us know how the land lies when you get there. Have a good look around the property if it's quiet, if it looks like there is anyone in the property get in touch.'

'Will do.'

'Any news from Paula and Simon yet?'

'Not yet, I'll get them to contact you when they're back,' Emma replied.

'Great, then they can get into Sammy's finances. Okay Scott, let's go and speak to Sammy's mother.'

'Right, She's in Billinge, near the Hare and Hounds, I know the quickest way to get there, we'll be there in 10 minutes.' Said Scott.

Ten minutes later they were parking up outside Anne Lomas' bungalow.

'I'll go in by myself Scott, I don't want to appear as if we're mob handed and scare her.'

Steve rang the doorbell and the door was quickly opened by a sprightly lady in her early seventies.

'Hello, Mrs Lomas, I'm a friend and colleague of your son, Sammy. I work for the Police in Wigan; I'm Detective Inspector Steve Wicks and I'm trying to get hold of Sammy regarding a question I have about a recent autopsy he performed for us. I'm struggling to get hold of him. I'm sure he's fine, I believe he's having a short break, a few days away, he forgot to tell anyone where he was going and his phone appears to be struggling to pick up a signal.'

'Come in, come in.' Said Mrs Lomas, 'You'll catch your death out there it's so cold.

'Thank you, it is a bit cold, must be the elevation in Billinge making it colder,' Steve said.

'It is colder here, that's true.' Steve followed Mrs Lomas into the living room where a log burner was keeping the temperature more than cosy

'It's not like Sammy to not let me know he was going away. I spoke to him yesterday on the phone and he didn't mention anything about taking a break. He sounded well though.'

'I'm glad he's safe and well, that's good to know. You don't have any idea where he might have gone by any chance, for a few days of peace and quiet, do you?' Asked Steve.

'Well he does have his place up in Grasmere that he recently bought so he could go walking and fishing. It's just a short drive up the M6, such a beautiful part of the world and on our doorstep too. I don't understand his desire to go fishing. Don't get me wrong it's a lovely place but too remote if you ask me,'

'If he calls again, could you tell him that his friend Steve is trying to get in touch with him urgently.'

'I will dear. I know he'll be keen to help you if he can, let me make a note of your name.'

'No need Mrs Lomas, here's my card just in case he calls you. It's quite important that we speak but I know the phone signal isn't always great if he's in the Lake District. I'll get out of your way now and let you get on with your day.

'Okay dear, I'll let him know, he rings me regularly.'

'Thank you, Mrs Lomas, you stay sat down, I'll let myself out,' said Steve.

When he got back into the car Sott asked if they were any closer to finding Sammy.

'Well we now know that he was in contact with his mother yesterday and he didn't mention he was taking a few days off work, which she said was unusual but that was all. She did back up that he'd recently bought a place in the Lake District and that it was remote. Sounds like a good place to hide someone. I just don't think finding Jude is going to be that easy. Sammy has a logical brain; he knows how we work. I'm guessing he will have thought it through in his head many times and come up with something more complex than that. It worries me that we don't know what his next move is likely to be. Are we going to find Jude as another murder victim and Sammy has disappeared? He's capable, I'm just hoping that when he finds out we're looking for him he'll give Jude up alive and well.'

'He has no reason to kill Jude. I know it's very likely that he killed our 2 murder victims but those acts were fuelled by revenge. Jude disappearing isn't an act of revenge. It's an act of someone who could see the walls closing in. I think when he's worked out what his next move is he'll probably let Jude go. Everyone I've spoken to has said he seemed like a solid, stand-up good guy. He's got himself into something and Jude has taken his control away from him. Nobody, not even Jude, saw this coming. You say he's got a logical strong mind so he surely must know he can't get away with this,' said Scott.

'Push a rat into a corner though Scott and it doesn't just give up and wait for its fate. It goes on the attack; it fights for its life; it goes for your throat. I thought I understood who Sammy was but now I don't know if he's a rat or a mouse. His attack involves Jude and that's gone way too far. You're right though, you would have to think that, if he was in his right mind, he couldn't have thought he'd possibly get away with this. But if he isn't in his right mind, he's more dangerous than anyone could have thought possible. He's obviously a long way out of his right mind.'

'Let's hope he realises he can't get away with it and contacts us soon guv, I just don't think him not contacting us to let us know he has Jude feels in any way right guv,' replied Scott.

Steve heard his mobile phone signal an incoming email and asked Scott to drive back to the station and got his phone out of his jacket pocket.

To : Steve Wicks
From : Anonymous
Subject : Jude Lawler
DI Wicks

Thank you for informing me of my other brother's death. As you are probably aware already, I will not lose any sleep over that news. He was always a loser, a disappointment to the whole family, so it comes as no surprise to me that he ended up taking his own life. He will not be missed, he meant nothing to me. Consider your duty of informing the next of kin as completed.

I'm sorry to hear about your DS. My thoughts are no doubt the same as yours. My mother and brothers killer has now made it very personal to you. Step very carefully from now on. I think you need to look closer to home for help. If I was in your shoes I would be looking to your sister. She has access to intelligence sources that the Police just don't even know about yet, let alone have access to it, and all that comes with specialist backup.

I have thought long and hard about who the killer may be but can't point a finger at anybody. I will stop there and that is as much as I can say on the subject. I wish you well catching the killer. I was very close to my mother, not as close to my brother Dave and as for Simon I have no more words to waste on him.

Anonymous

Chapter Twenty-One

John loved the Lake District; the splendour and magnificence still astounded him. He'd enjoyed the drive up the M6 motorway then through the A roads past Kendal, Lake Windermere, Rydal Water, Ambleside and on to Grasmere. The roads had been quiet and he'd been able to put his foot down. It still amazed him that he lived on the doorstep of one of the most beautiful places in the world. What amazed him even more was that he knew people from Wigan who had never visited the Lake District, never seen the spectacular scenery, never breathed the fresh air or walked the paths that lead to most spectacular views. It had taken him 90 minutes to get to Grasmere, he knew the route like the back of his hand, he was hiking in the Lake District as often as the job allowed. He'd been coming here since before he could walk, with his parents, his father carrying him around in a baby carrier until he was strong enough to walk the hills by himself.

John parked up in Grasmere and put on his walking boots in the car park, his walking coat and an Arab shemag scarf that he could pull up over his face and head and not look too out of place. It was a great disguise and warm in the winter weather. He was dressed head to foot in black and not many people he knew would have known who he was without studying his gait. He decided to do a walk past Sammy's place initially to check for any sign of his car and any sign of anyone being inside. There were no lights on and no smoke coming out of the chimneys. Nothing to make him think that anybody was inside. He'd walked past the house hundreds of times over the years, he never imagined he'd have it under surveillance at any time in the future.

He made the decision that he'd break in to the house when it went dark. Grasmere was quiet and Sammy's holiday place was no different. Sammy's place was about half a mile away from the centre of the village so as a place to bring a kidnapping victim it was perfect. He made his way to a café in the village and decided to call Steve to give him an update.

'Hi guv,' said John, 'I'm just calling to give you an update.'
'Okay, thanks John, what have you seen?'

'It's all very quiet guv, no sign of any vehicle parked up. There is an old cement mixer around the back which suggests Sammy is having some work done but no sign of any tradesmen. I figured I'd leave it a couple of hours until it goes dark then force the back door and have a look round. If Jude is here, I need to get in there and hope Sammy isn't, but if he is I'll overpower him and make the arrest.'

'Go in now John, don't wait, we need to get it ticked off the list and get you back here for an early start tomorrow.'

'Okay guv, I'll let you know how I get on.'

'Don't worry about the break in, you tried several times to get the owners attention and Jude is in danger of her life from a murder suspect, nobody will complain and if they do, we talked it through and I gave you instructions to do what you're going to do.'

'I was doing it anyway, but thanks guv.'

When he got back to his car, he picked up a 24-inch pry bar from his boot that he'd used the year before to take down his old kitchen. He'd thought he could use it on any obstacles he came across so he'd come tooled up, just like the criminals he was paid to arrest... It wouldn't look good if he was caught but it was a colleagues life in danger. He knew what he had to do and he'd worry about the consequences later. He put the pry bar in his rucksack and made his way back to Sammy's house.

Making sure nobody was on the road he made his way down the side of the house. Everything was quiet. The house was typical of the area, built of slate stone along with the garden walls. A very nice house but obviously not fully to Sammy's liking as he was having work done. He could see the cement mixer he'd seen earlier along with a builders locked up container, probably being used for storage of tools and materials. He had a quick look through the windows at the back of the house and there was no sign of life. He didn't expect to see anything on the ground floor, if Jude was here she'd be in a bedroom with a gag on and probably chained to a wall or floor.

He forced the pry bar between the door and the frame and forced it home. Gripping it tightly he pushed it with all his strength. He surprised himself by gaining entrance on the first attempt. 'Sammy, if you're not our killer I apologise for the door but I'm sure you'll understand under the circumstances,' thought John, 'your back door was crap and you're going to need a new one fitting...or maybe not...if you're our killer you'll probably never see this place again.'

John took a few seconds to catch his breath, his heart rate was up and his testosterone was pumping through his body too. He needed to get himself under control or he'd do some damage if Sammy was here. It was still light enough to see so he had to be careful, he didn't want to be Sammy's next victim. He kept hold of the pry bar as a weapon. The kitchen was virtually empty apart from a cooker and a small fridge still in place. All the previous units and worktops had been ripped out and removed off site already.

The house was an average size, 3 bedrooms, Kitchen, living room, dining room, bathroom and toilet with decent sized gardens front and back. A garden shed with a log store and a greenhouse to the back of the house completed the buildings that he would need to check on.

There were a few chairs in the living room, probably used by the builders for tea breaks other than the chairs it was very sparse and cold. It was obviously a house that Sammy was having work done to over the winter to use come spring and summer.

John spent about fifteen minutes looking in every room for signs of Jude, any clues that she had been here. There was no cellar and the cupboard under the stairs had just a few empty cardboard boxes in it. Upstairs he opened the door to the roof space using the pole and hook that was nearby. A ladder automatically dropped down and John popped his head into the roof space and looked around it with the help of his torch. It was probably the tidiest roof space he'd ever seen, no boxes of clothes, no kids toys, nothing that people use a storage space for. It was as empty as when it had been built. The previous owners had probably hired a skip and emptied everything out of the roof space directly into the skip. It took John probably twenty seconds to decide that the house had no signs of Jude or Sammy. The greenhouse, the shed and the builders storage container still needed to be checked but he didn't fancy Jude's chances if she was in any of those in this weather. He was fine because he was dressed for the weather in the best of waterproof and breathable hiking gear along with head cover and gloves, he was also able to move around to get his temperature up, he doubted Jude had the same ability.

He made his way to the shed first, there was no lock on the door and when he opened it the shed was empty. Next he looked at the greenhouse, again it was completely empty, not even a single plant pot, the last thing to look at was the builders container.

John walked around the container, looking for any signs of life. There was nothing he could see that screamed at him so he attacked the two locks with the help of his trusty pry bar. The locks were better than the lock on the back door but even so, within thirty seconds the two locks were on the floor. He couldn't help thinking that the crime rate in Cumbria must be a lot less than in Wigan if the locks people thought necessary were so weak, he'd forced three locks in no time at all. He kept hold of the pry bar, not knowing what he'd see on the inside of the container. He opened the door and shone his torch into the space. It was full of kitchen units stacked on top of each other. No room to keep anybody locked up. He could see to the back of the container; it was only small. He took the time to check the inside of the units just in case he was actually looking for a body but within ten minutes he was sure that there was nothing in there apart from kitchen units and some tools ready for the team that would be fitting them.

He closed the door leaving the locks on the floor. If nothing else came from his visit to Grasmere at least the builders might buy better locks in future. He felt so disappointed though, they still hadn't found Jude or Sammy and Sammy must know that he's now on their radar and there was no sign of him coming quietly…there was no sign of him at all.

When he got back to his car he took off his walking boots and put his trainers back on. He then rang Steve to let him know what he'd found.

'Hi guv, neither Sammy or Jude were there. No sign of much inside the house to be honest, empty apart from a few chairs. It's obviously being renovated; the kitchen is at least, but other than that the house is empty. I checked everywhere the place was eerily empty if I'm being honest.'

'What about the builders container?' asked Steve.

'Full of high-end kitchen units and I had a good look, Jude wasn't there guv and no sign that she'd been there and then moved on.'

'Okay john, thanks for that, at least we can cross it off the list, get yourself back here.'

'Will do, how are things going back there any good news?'

'Unfortunately not, we've just got warrants to enter any properties owned by Sammy so you were covered to do what you did, no issues there.'

'I think if Jude had been there she would have been able to break her way out, the locks weren't exactly up to much, one strong kick and they'd give up the battle.'

'Forensics are currently at Sammy's main property in Wigan with some uniforms helping the search. I'm going over there with Scott to have a look then we'll be back at base for a meeting to see where we're up to as a team and sort out what our next moves are.'

'Okay boss, I'll set off back now, should be back in an hour and a half.'

***

'Thanks everyone, it's been a very busy day today and we need to share what we've found so far to give us the direction for tonight and tomorrow,' said Steve. 'John, would you start by telling us what you found in Grasmere.'

'It's one we can cross off our list for now. There was no sign of Jude or Sammy and no sign that they'd been there. The place was a bit of a building site to be honest, hardly any furniture. A bit bleak when you look at it, so easy to search. That's not to say it won't be used in the near future, as a place to hide Jude and keep us busy if Sammy's making a run for it.'

'Good point John, I'll contact Cumbria police and ask them to keep a regular eye on the place, maybe I'll ask them to call into the property every day for the next few days to see if there's any signs of habitation. It's definitely a property of interest and we shouldn't get any problems from Cumbria Police seeing as how the kidnapped person is a DS. I know they've got a large area to cover but I don't think we'll have an issue with them. Thanks John. Finances next, Emma, what have we found out?'

'Sammy's finances are complex; he has a lot of income streams and a lot of outgoings that go along with those incomes. He has many bank accounts, one for his rental properties, one for the lecturing work he does at Manchester University, one that he seems to use for his classic car hobby, one he uses for his pathology income, many ISA accounts and managed fund accounts. He's so rich it's eyewatering and financially he knows what he's doing. Probably learned it from his cousin, David Burns. There hasn't been any movement out of those accounts, apart from historical direct debits, in the last 4 days. No credit card use, but before that he did make some large cash withdrawals within the last 2 months. One for £10,000, one for £5,000 and a lot of ATM cash withdrawals which stopped 4 days ago. Whatever he's doing he's been planning it since long before the murders. Worryingly I'd say it points to him being ready to run.'

'Thanks Emma, do we have requests for notifications of debit and credit card use in future?' asked Steve.

'We do, if he tries to use anything other than cash we'll know about it immediately. I don't know about any foreign banks he's using yet though guv, they take more time to come through and there's so many more to consider.'

'Keep on asking the questions. Maybe look at any foreign trips Sammy has made over the last 5 years and look at banks from those countries for bank accounts in Sammy's name. At least if he makes a mistake and uses any of his UK cards we'll know about it'

'Paula and Simon, how did you get on today?' asked Steve.

'We went to Sammy's main residence firstly,' replied Paula, 'nothing out of place from the outside. His daily drive wasn't on the road or the drive but we could see it in the garage along with several other cars. We've got a list of cars he owns though and Simon has printed off a list for us and uniforms to try to locate. There are 2 cars we can't locate as yet; one is a 2004 Bentley Continental and the other is a 1963 Rolls Royce Silver Cloud. In my opinion neither of these cars, nice though they are, would be the type of car in which you could shrink into the background. He may have sold them for cash but unlikely as they are worth big money or he's having them transported abroad to start a new life in the sun. Bentley his everyday drive and the Rolls Royce because it means so much to him he can't bear to be without it. We can look at the history of the vehicles and if anything stands out. We're trying to find a vehicle he might have purchased over the past few days but nothing is jumping out at us as yet but when we do find one we'll look at ANPR to see where it's been hitting.'

'Good idea, put the Bentley and the Rolls Royce on the ANPR system too, before you finish for today,' said Steve 'I've been with Scott most of the day and I think Scott will agree with me when I say it's been as frustrating a day as we've ever come across. Everything I've heard from you all tells me that Sammy is definitely our man as far as the murders are concerned but I feel like I'm missing something when it comes to Jude. The answer will come, probably while I'm making a brew at home at 2am because I can't sleep. On that I'm going to call it a day after I've seen DCI Greenwood. Let your subconscious work on the answers at home. It's important when we've had a busy day and we're not getting a break that we relax, get a good sleep and see if our subconscious works on the case overnight. With that it's been a busy, tiring day already, just get your desks straight for today, get any requests you need to put in done then get off home. Come back tomorrow morning. I don't want to see any of you still here when I get out of the DCI's office. We haven't got the answers we need but I still feel like today has been a good day. I'll see you all tomorrow.'

Steve left the main office and headed towards Dave Greenwoods office. As he expected Dave was still there, even though he'd been in since first thing this morning.

'Hello Steve, come and sit down. How are things going with finding Sammy?' asked Dave.

'Frustrating to be honest. There's something I'm not quite grasping but it will come. We've not found Jude yet but we've got another big day tomorrow. I wanted to ask about getting the press involved, maybe the local press to start with, asking anyone who's seen Jude or Sammy over the last 2 days to get in touch. What do you think?'

'I've been thinking the same thing myself. I don't think we've got anything to lose. We'll get some calls we'll have to deal with from the crazy brigade but if we don't put it out on a full moon and we get the right person taking the calls we should be able to filter out most of the crazies. I'll get in touch with the press officer and let him loose on it. I'll let you know when I've set something up so you can be involved,' said Dave. 'You look shattered Steve, don't go running on empty. I know under the circumstances it's not easy but you need to look after yourself. Why don't you get off home, see if you can come up with that missing piece to the puzzle. It doesn't always happen when you're sat at your desk. You know how these things work.'

'I do boss, I've just told my team pretty much the same thing,' said Steve. 'I am tired, it's been a long, frustrating day but I do get the feeling we're not too far away.'

'Okay Steve, I'll see you tomorrow.'

***

Steve drove home in a bit of a daze and on autopilot, he couldn't even remember getting in his car. When he entered his apartment he shouted Angie's name but got no answer. five minutes later he heard the key in the lock and Angie coming in.

'Hi Steve, your car was parked in its usual spot so I figured you were here. How did your day go? Asked Angie.

'Hi Angie, not great. We've not found any sign of Jude and Sammy appears to have disappeared into the ether. The longer this goes on for the lower our chances are of finding her.'

Angie took her coat off and walked through to the kitchen with Steve at her heals, 'I'll put the kettle on, I'm parched.'

Steve had his phone in his hands and got his emails on screen, opening the latest one from Paul Worrall.

'I got this email, have a look at it and give me your thoughts on it,' Steve said handing his mobile phone over to Angie, 'I'll make us a drink, hot chocolate? I know you love it on a day like today.'

'Ooh yes please,' replied Angie looking at the phone. She read the email twice before giving Steve any sort of reply. 'What he says is true, I do have access to intelligence sources you don't have access to as a police officer and yes I do have specialist backup. Very specialised, but I am not allowed to use the intelligence sources for anything other than for the work I do for the intelligence service I'm attached to…

'So you can't help me find Jude, even though you might have information available at your fingertips.'

'I didn't say that Steve, you didn't let me finish. I was about to say that the head of the Manchester office also happens to be my partner. I'm working out of The Hague, attached to Europol because it was seen an unsustainable relationship given our work. We were both working out of London when the issue of our relationship arose and I found myself attached to Europol very quickly. My partner, James, was sent to head up the Manchester office. I fully understand the relationship issues yourself and Jude have found yourself with but I also have a very good friend who may be in a position to bend the rules…no promises but our time with this particular intelligence agency is probably coming to a natural end and we could use Paul Worrall's position in your case as a way to be able to help you.'

'I can't ask for any more than that. I'm not going to ask what you can do but Jude has become even more important to me since she went missing. I can't lose her so anything you can do to help. I trust you to do whatever you can. Thank you.'

'I hadn't seen my partner for 18 months. Meeting up again in Manchester was very difficult, emotionally, but we have a shared need, desire, call it whatever you like. We opened our hearts and both wanted the same thing, a simpler life. I'm here to help you as much as I can but I'll be very much in the background.'

'I won't ask anything else. To know you're doing your thing, whatever that is, means everything to me.'

'Good, as far as you're concerned I'm continuing working on bringing Paul Worrall to justice and neutralising his ability to threaten the nation's security. Our paths just happened to cross along our separate journeys.'

'Got it, now do you want cream on top of your hot chocolate?'

'You don't really have to ask that, of course I do,' replied Angie with a smile on her face which was there because she felt like a big weight had been lifted from her shoulders.

Chapter Twenty-Two

The team were in early the next day and busy carrying on from where they had left off the day before.

'John, get your coat, we're going back to Sammy's house, what we need to know has probably been staring us in the face, we just don't know what it is yet.' Said Steve.

'Ok guv, I agree, if he's been planning this as long as we believe he must have left a clue somewhere, Sammy's house has to be favourite for where that clue might be,' replied John.

'You drive, I need to think.'

John didn't spare the horses on the way to Sammy's house. The rear door had been forced and temporarily boarded over from the first police entry into the house. A substantial padlock had been fitted to make it safe. Steve produced the padlock key from his pocket and they were in.

'This is some house Sammy has got, even in his work position and with other income sources it's very impressive, far too big for one person though.' Said John.

'He hasn't always lived here by himself you know, Jane lived here for nearly 3 years. Sammy was as happy as I've ever seen while she was here. She seemed to complete him. It must have felt like kick in the guts when they found out about Jane's stage 4 cancer diagnosis. Death of a loved one can affect people very differently. I thought Sammy was doing really well, he threw himself into work, his cars and lecturing at Manchester University. It was the only way I survived for quite a long time. It does catch up with you though, you can't dodge grief, it changes who you are. Sammy could have been planning the murders of the Worrall's since before Jane's death and nobody knew. If Jane hadn't died the Worrall's may well still be alive. I can't believe it was a snap decision, this has been festering. Now let's look for anything that will point us in the right direction. Let's start in the master bedroom. We had better put gloves and shoe covers on, treat this place like a crime scene.'

Sammy had good taste in his furnishings and decorating his home, or had it been Jane? She had definitely lived here long enough for a whirlwind of a woman, like she had been, to make a massive difference in a short time. Everything in the house looked high end and it looked perfect in such a grand house.

Steve opened up the door within the master bedroom which led to a large walk-in wardrobe. Jane's clothes were still there, all neatly hung, colourful and looking fresh to wear. Steve understood this. It had taken him years to start emptying his house of Kim and Mia's clothes and even now he kept 2 large suitcases full of clothes. He just couldn't bring himself to totally get rid of the physical things. He knew he had the memories they had all contributed to but he needed something more.

He was beginning to feel again the despair that Sammy had felt. Luckily Steve had been able to overcome the despair, he knew he would never fully move on from Kim and Mia's deaths. He and Jude had spoken of this before they had got together. Jude had totally understood that they were a massive part of his life and she didn't believe he ever had to fully move on. She even doubted anyone in Steve's position could ever fully move on from such a tragedy. Like any relationship there was give and take on both parts. Steve had parked his grief, after enough time that he felt able to move on. His grief would always be part of his life, getting smaller and smaller year on year but never fully leaving. Jude understood that and it was thinking like this that had brought them both to a moment of clarity. They were getting closer as time went on, to the point where neither of them could deny their needs for a loving relationship. They understood each other so well; Sammy being older than Steve possibly believed he would never come to a moment in his life, or what remained of his life, where he would be able to move on.

'It's been staring us in the face the whole time, clear as day, Jane was the straw that broke the camel's back. He can't bring himself to get rid of anything that she touched...I should have seen this before now.'

Steve got his mobile phone out of his jacket pocket and rang Emma.

'Hi Emma, I need you to drop what you're doing and find out the address or addresses of any properties Jane Smythe owned before she died. She was Sammy's fiancé and died nearly 3 years ago. I'm guessing Sammy hasn't been able to put it up for sale or has bought it off her son's without going through solicitors and without changing the name on the deeds.'

'I'm on it now guv,' replied Emma, 'I'll get back to you when I find anything.'

Steve rang off and John was watching him. Steve had found the missing link; John was sure of it. Steve understood that the missing link came from a place of love. He probably only understood this because of the tragedy he'd suffered in his life. He also understood that when a person reaches a crossroad, like Sammy had with the murder of his cousin in prison and latterly with the death of Jane, his soulmate, there are several paths you can take. Most paths are good. Sammy had chosen, if it was in fact a choice, the wrong path. He'd killed at least two people and kidnapped another. If this was the case Steve would never admit to anyone the fact that he could understand Sammy's actions. He also knew that Jude was still alive. Jude's only mistake had been to get too close to the truth, she hadn't been part of the reason that Sammy was such a broken man. Sammy had already meted out retribution by killing Dave and Karen Worrall. There was nothing he could do to revenge Jane's death, Jane died not at the hands of others, if anything he would blame himself for his inability to save her. By the time she had her diagnosis she was living on borrowed time while the unforgiving disease spread quickly to her brain, liver, bones and adrenal glands. He had no reason to kill Jude but they needed to find her quickly, because, having found some retribution for the killing of his cousin, and Jane's untimely death he might now believe that he had no reason to continue… Job done!!

Steve and John had moved from the master bedroom to Sammy's study. There was so much now, looking through eyes that understood Sammy's issues, that everywhere they looked was a shrine to Jane. He still had Jane's coats hung in the cloakroom by the front door. Neither Steve or John had seen it before but it was clear that Sammy would make a decision soon and finding Jude quickly had now become an even bigger priority, if that was even possible.

Steve's mobile phone rang and he could see it was Emma calling.

'Guv, you were right, Jane Smythe is still down as the owner of a property off Winstanley Road. A converted barn with no neighbours within 200 metres.' She sent John the address via WhatsApp.

'Thanks Emma, great work. Myself and John are on our way there now. Can you put me through to DCI Greenwood.'

'Transferring now guv.'

'Steve, any news on Jude?' said Dave Greenwood.

'Yes boss, we've found a house where Jude might be. Sammy's fiancé Jane, who died, as you know, nearly 3 years ago is still the owner on the deeds to the property. Sammy probably felt no desire to sell it on. It's easy to get to but quite a distance to the nearest neighbour so would make a good fit to keep a kidnapping victim without raising too many concerns. Myself and John are just about to set out now.'

'Okay Steve, keep me updated. I'm going to arrange an armed response team, considering we're dealing with a murderer.'

'I think that's a wise move, but having said that I also think that Sammy has already done everything he wanted to regarding what he set out to do.'

'Okay, I'll get a four-man team out there anyway. We don't exactly know the state of Sammy's mind. They'll be in an unmarked car. Wait until they get there before proceeding with the search. I know you'll want to get in there and rescue Jude, if she's there, but an extra ten minutes isn't going to make any difference. Wait for armed response.'

'Okay boss, we'll be waiting.'

With the phone call ended, Steve and John got in the car and made the 10-minute drive from Sammy's house having resecured Sammy's house before leaving.

'Park up just before the track on the left. We'll wait here for the armed response team, if they aren't here in ten minutes we're going in...Agreed?' Asked Steve.

'Agreed.' Replied John. It's exactly what John had expected Steve to say. Jude could be within reach, there was no way they weren't going in, armed back up or not.

Eight minutes later a black BMW X5 parked up behind them and behind the armed response vehicle Scott's blue Vauxhall

Astra parked up with Emma in the passenger seat. Both Scott and Emma were wearing overt body armour.

Steve and John got out of Steve's car, John to get the body armour out of the boot while Steve went to tell the armed response unit how he wanted the next ten minutes to play out. Steve then walked over to Scott's car.

'You couldn't keep away then?' said Steve.

'She's one of our team guv…try keeping us away,' said Scott.

'Thanks you two, I appreciate it, let's hope she's here. Follow us in at the rear and block the exit then follow down on foot. I don't expect Sammy to be here but you never know.'

'We thought you'd appreciate the back-up guv, you know me, anything for the chance of a dust up. Take us in, we're right behind you.'

'Just give me a few seconds to get my armoured vest on then we're going in.'

One minute later three cars pulled into the grounds of the barn conversion. One blocking the exit and the other two pulling up in front, skidding on the gravel driveway. If someone was in the house they certainly knew they had visitors now. The four armed response officers were out of the car first. Two to the front door with Steve and John and two around the back followed by Scott and Emma.

'Open the door, armed police officers.' No response from inside.

'Open the door, armed police officers.' Again no response.

'Use the big red key, let's get in there.' One of the armed response guys pulled the battering ram up to the front door and on the third blow the door flew open. The battering ram was discarded and the armed police entered the house. A similar scene was happening at the rear door and all four- armed police were in the house checking off each room for signs of life and quickly giving the all-clear sign.

'Scott, Emma, start a quick search in here, see if there are any signs that Jude has been here. John, follow me, let's see what there is in the way of outbuildings. You two help the search and you two come with me and John.' Steve said to the armed officers. No time to learn names, he was sure they'd understand.

They went out of the back door, the armed officers carrying their pistols in front of them. The grounds were big, about an acre of garden which considering the owner had been dead for nearly three years were in remarkably good condition. The outbuildings consisted of a shed, a greenhouse and a stable block big enough for two horses.

'John, check out the shed and greenhouse, I'll check the stables.'

One armed officer followed Steve and the other followed John. The stables had stopped being stables a long time ago judging by the inside. It looked as though the internal walls that made it into a stable block had been removed and it had probably been used as a garage and tool store. There was also a ride on lawn mower but there was no sign of Jude.

As soon as Steve stepped out of the stables he felt overwhelming disappointment. He had been sure he'd find Jude here. It was a quiet garden, there was the low hum of the M6 motorway which passed within a quarter of mile of the back fence but not much else. He then heard a banging sound and walked around the back of the stables. Then he heard a cry for help. He found a small container which had been skilfully hidden by bushes and trees.

'Jude, is that you?' Steve asked while banging on the container door.

'Yes, please get me out of here.'

'Give me a minute to find something to get into the container.'

Steve shouted John over, 'she's in the well-hidden container, behind the stables. Help me find something to break the padlock off.' They quickly found a sledge hammer. 'This will work guv. Let's get her out.' John brought the sledgehammer down in one smooth motion and it surrendered first time.

Scott and Emma had heard the commotion and had come to see what was happening just as the door was opened flooding the container with daylight. Jude covered her eyes against the light, she hadn't seen daylight for a few days but she could only guess how long that had been. Steve was hugging Jude within seconds and asking if she was okay.

'Steve, I've never been so happy to see anyone before in my life. I knew you'd get to me. Where am I by the way?' Jude was in tears; she could see the whole team was here and had never felt as connected to a team as she did now. 'I'm okay, I think, desperate for a hot shower, and a good meal and a nice soft bed to sleep in. Get me out of here, there's a key just by the door, I'm guessing it'll fit the lock on this shackle.' John got the key and handed it to Steve. It fitted the lock and she was free once more.

'John, get a forensic team down here, we need to know it's Sammy who did this,' said Steve.

'It's Sammy alright, it's started coming back to me what happened.'

'John, you stay here, get the forensics team working. Secure the house and grounds, look for anything that points to Sammy and search for the murder weapon.'

DCI Greenwood walked through the house to where Jude and the team were standing. 'Great to see you Jude, great work everyone. How are you feeling?' He asked Jude.

'Considering I've been in a metal box that was at one time used to store hay and horse feed for God knows how long I'm remarkably okay, relieved. Nobody has been here for 24 hours, I'm guessing. But considering I've still got lots of sandwiches and water I'm guessing nobody was due to come today.'

'Steve, get Jude back to your place, I'll get the police doctor to call round to check you over.'

'I just want to get some hot food, a comfy bed and some time to think things through.'

'Take care of her Steve, the doctor will be there within the hour and then you can relax. Steve I don't want you in the station tomorrow, look after Jude. And Jude I don't want to see you in the station until you're ready to come back in.'

'Thanks boss, do we have any idea where Sammy is?'

'Steve you can answer any questions Jude has regarding the case but I'm guessing looking at the CCTV cameras on the back and front of the house Sammy will probably know now what has happened. I reckon he'll go on the run but we'll be looking at that, don't worry Jude we'll get him, leave Sammy to us for now. We've done the most important bit of the job by finding you. He won't get away from us that easily.'

With that Steve helped Jude into his car, Sammy wasn't taking priority at that moment in time. Like his DCI said, they'd done the most important thing in getting Jude back safely. He now wanted to look after her and he knew whatever happened from this point forward she would be a big part of his life.

Chapter Twenty-Three

The doctor gave Jude the all clear, physically, but advised she see a counsellor for the sake of her mental health; she had been living in a shipping container for four days, in fear for her life, after all. He said the best thing she could do would be to process what had happened while taking long walks in the fresh air, open up to someone, Steve if not a trained counsellor. She needed to get her feelings out in the open and be proactive about her recovery.

Jude was just so happy to be back with Steve: she knew she'd made a mistake, and as it turned out a big mistake. If she'd waited for Steve, to just let him know about her findings into Sammy, instead of disbelieving herself and thinking she must be wrong, Sammy would now be locked up for the murders of Dave and Karen Worrall and life would be just fine and dandy. That's not to say that life wouldn't be fine and dandy anyway, it was just a little less certain now as it had been four days ago.

'How are you feeling now you've seen a doctor?' asked Steve.

'I'm fine, apart from the aches and pains of sleeping on an uncomfortably thin mattress, chained to a steel wall with limited movements. I'll get over that in no time, it's nothing that a nice hot bath, some decent food and a sleep in a comfortable bed can't sort out. I'll be fine Steve, I don't bear a grudge towards Sammy, in his mind he did what he had to do when confronted by the reality of his situation. I don't believe he would ever hurt me in any way. I never felt in danger, I was drugged up to my eyeballs by Sammy to keep me compliant. I do bear a grudge towards Sammy for being a double murderer though.'

'I know it's Sammy we're talking about and it feels a little unbelievable,' Steve said, 'but he kidnapped you don't forget, locked you up for four days. We were all out of our minds with worry. I thought I was going to lose you before we had a proper chance at a life. It was really pointless Sammy keeping hold of you once we knew he was the killer, but he did, he must have been keeping all options open. I bear a grudge towards him and I'll do everything I can to put him behind bars'.

'I think he did something so out of his comfort zone that he acted way out of character. I'm not making any excuse for him but the loss of two major people who were so important in his life was probably just one too many.'

'Don't forget I lost two major people in my life Jude, I didn't go on a killing spree, even though at times I felt like it.'

'Steve there's nobody who knows better than me what you went through and I would never belittle the struggle you had coming to terms with it. You know I love you with no conditions attached. I know what a truly good man you are. My kidnapping came to nothing. I'm safe, you're safe and in my mind that's all that matters at this moment in time. Let's not ponder too much on what ifs and maybes. I love you more now than I did four days ago. I knew you would find me. There was a moment early on after I'd been kidnapped when I thought we may never be together again, but here we are.'

'You are a truly amazing woman Jude, the thought of losing you after having just truly found you, after all this time, was killing me inside, but like you said, here we are.' Steve said with a huge smile on his handsome face.

Jude thought his smile was adorable, a window into his soul, a soul filled with so much love, her heart melted at the sight of it. Strange things happened when you were in the early stages of a relationship. Jude's experience over the last four days had cemented their feelings for each other. She knew everything would be incredible because of and not despite of those four days.

'Let me run you a hot bath then I'll order some food. What do you fancy, Indian, Chinese, Italian, Turkish, fish and chips?'

'Turkish, I have a need for meat and lots of it to build me up. Sandwiches are fine but I don't want to see another Marks and Spencer's sandwich for the rest of the year.'

'Oh, one more thing...the team knows about us. I thought I'd better mention it to Dave Greenwood considering the circumstances. I outed us, I hope you don't mind.'

'I thought you had when Dave told you to bring me back here and look after me...would have been a big ask if we weren't a thing. We'll deal with that going forward. I don't think it will be an issue but let's not try to fix the world in one conversation.

How's that bath coming along? Have you ordered the food yet?' Jude was smiling again; everything was going to work out fine.

Just then they both heard someone put a key in the apartment door and enter. It was Angie, when she walked in and saw Jude she was thrilled. They hugged then Angie turned to Steve, 'did you not think to call me little brother and let me know this beautiful woman had been found and was now safe and well?'

Steve and Jude both knew it was not a reprimand, it was more a 'look what happened, isn't it fantastic!' statement.

'Well, we found Jude about an hour ago. You were next on my list of people to inform.' He said winking at Jude.

'Your parents must be thrilled,' said Angie, 'They must have been out of their minds with worry.'

'They were, they're coming here tomorrow, they know I'm fine and that Steve's looking after me. Steve's going to be ordering a feast from the Turkish.'

'I'm not stopping, I just popped in to get changed then I'm out again. I'm in the UK so little these days that when I am here it feels like I have so many people to catch up with and you don't want me interfering with your evening. Make sure he treats you like a Princess or he'll have me to answer to.' Angie replied. 'We can catch up tomorrow if you'd like.'

'That sounds perfect, I only have the strength for a bath and food and I'm not sure I'll make it through both of them before I nod off.'

'Your bath awaits my Princess.' Said Steve.

'Perfect, we'll talk tomorrow Angie.'

***

Angie managed to sneak out, having got a change of clothes, leaving Steve and Jude to be alone. They didn't need Angie there. Angie had been involved in five kidnapping cases in her past. Not that Steve and Jude would ever know but in reality she was more qualified than Steve at mopping up the remains of a kidnapping situation. Now that Jude was safe she wanted to make sure that particular set of skills were put to good use again.

Chapter Twenty-Four

'Jamie, I'm coming over to yours for the evening,' Angie said, 'Jude has been found safe and well. Do we still have eyes on our guy?'

'We do and I've got two assets primed and ready to go, currently in the back of a transit van parked on the car park of the hotel, where the miscreant is no doubt planning his next move. You've worked with these two assets before. There will be no issues with their work.'

'Good, I'll be with you in 20 minutes, we can go through the plan one last time then we can go out for a meal, somewhere busy, with lots of internal cameras that can place us there tonight. I take it the operation is going ahead tonight.'

'It is my dear, I'll see if I can get us a table at the Ivy, I know the manager, when she finds out I'm bringing my lady she'll make a fuss of us both.'

'Sounds perfect Jamie.' Said Angie before breaking the connection. Twenty minutes later Angie parked her hire car in the basement car park attached to the apartment block Jamie was currently using as his base. Five minutes later Angie was relaxing with a gin and tonic in her hand.

'Did we get into the Ivy?' Angie asked.

'We did,' replied Jamie, 'you'll enjoy it, I've been known to spend time there with heads of security before dignitaries pay a visit to the area, waving the flag for king and country. Mainly when Sheiks are visiting, the odd prince too. I get to discuss security measures with their heads of security whilst enjoying a nice lunch. I'm a regular there so getting a table wasn't really an issue.'

'I imagine you have to draw a line for these heads of security as to what they can do, but more importantly what they can't do.'

'That's correct, some people would bring in a small army, armed beyond many countries security budgets. Lots of money to be made in the private sector.'

'We'll be a big step closer to that when we've got this week out of the way.' Said Angie, 'Can we just go over the major planning issues regarding extraction, storage and delivery of the Doctor before we eat.'

'Of course,' replied Jamie, 'the miscreant is currently holed up in a medium sized, medium quality hotel room in Preston, handy for motorway access. Our two assets have already hacked the internal and external hotel cameras and have a camera showing the corridor where his room is. Before the extraction they will take out the hotel's CCTV cameras for a ten-minute period, plenty time for them to be in and out and driving away before they reconnect the cameras. They will stick to an agreed route to bring him to a safe house on the outskirts of Wigan. This route will be mainly through rural areas so they pass as few ANPR cameras as possible. During the drive they will change vehicles up to three times. All vehicles are in place, parked up out of sight of any cameras. When the time is right he will be transferred to the final destination and other agencies contacted. We've called in a few favours on this, strictly off the books and strictly with people I would trust my life with. Let's call it our last hoorah.'

'It all sounds really good so far,' said Angie.

'When it comes to the last transfer the assets will follow our plan to hold him, high on drugs but uncomfortably so, on the third night they will transfer him to the final destination where he will be anaesthetised and a message sent from his own phone to your brother's mobile telling him to come and get the clown. By that time we will be in London, having travelled there by train to discuss with our respective bosses how we see our futures going, which is out of the public sector. When that's all settled we come back to Manchester to set our new lives up as security consultants to the rich and famous,' replied Jamie, 'Our two assets are the perfect guys for this job. You'd want them on your team given the opportunity to get them and they have shown a desire to follow us into the private sector.'

'Get this one right with no hitches and it's a nailed-on position waiting for them.'

'You know my view on operations we've done in the past and will do in the future no doubt. We are the lesser of two evils. Sometimes we have to take matters into our own hands and we do it with good grace and a clear conscience because it is the right thing to do. We skirt the laws and sometimes break the laws because we come from a position of expertise. We always have and we always will.'

***

The evening at the Ivy was very enjoyable, the extraction, which would begin later that evening was never mentioned. Instead Angie and Jamie were like a couple of excited kids. They talked about their future together knowing that they'd been across many CCTV cameras in Manchester and there were excellent lip readers in the service who only needed to read a few wrong words on a security tape to make their lives very difficult.

They would be travelling to London in the morning for a couple of days, during which they would speak to the people who mattered, to discuss their futures and leaving their current employment. Having given a large portion of their lives to queen and country and latterly King and country, they saw no issues. They had been excellent representatives of the British Security Services but now was the right time to go, the right time for them to be together. It had always been on the cards that they would leave together; Angie's mother's death had been the final nail in the coffin, so to speak. They were both wealthy in their own right and decided to take a punt at setting up in Manchester, one of the cities that was very upwardly mobile with large investment into buildings and infrastructure. They had a phenomenal set of contacts within the industry within the North of England and had come up with a plan to go into the private sector in only a week. The operation that would shortly be in full flow was a tester, call it a nerve settler, and for Angie it had become personal when her brother's partner had been kidnapped.

Later that night operation kick start would be in full flow. It went without issue and Sammy had found himself being hauled in and out of several vehicles. He was barely aware though as he'd been drugged whilst still in his bed in Preston. It was only right that Sammy should have a taste of his own medicine, call it restorative justice for Jude.

In the small hours Sammy was offloaded into a darkened room with only a night light to see by. He was attached to a bracket in the ceiling via his wrists. He couldn't lie down, sit down or do anything much. In an hour he would be fully conscious but none the wiser.

Karma really was a bitch but who had done this to him, he would have no idea, he'd been as near to unconscious as he could be. He would remember nothing; he wouldn't know where he was or who had brought him here. When he did gain full consciousness and had a few minutes to gather his thoughts he grudgingly thought, 'Whoever you are I must say, well played.' This in his mind was only going one way, he'd killed two people from the same family. The chances were very high that he was now being held by 'friends' of that family and would probably end up with a big hole in the back of his head. He had to smile at this, whatever this was he hadn't planned how this was supposed to play out. He had nothing, he wasn't worried, however, he'd take whatever came his way and accept it. He knew his life was as good as over now. He felt calm about the consequences of his actions, he had lost so much in recent years that he never truly believed this whole endeavour would end up in his favour.

Chapter Twenty-Five

Steve woke the following morning early; the bedroom was warm and comfortable. Without opening his eyes he reached over for Jude but the emptiness and coldness of Jude's side of the bed sent Steve into a panic. He jumped out of his bed in one leap shouting Jude's name. Jude came rushing into the bedroom because Steve had sounded strained and panicked.

'What's the matter Steve? I'm here.'

'Jude…sorry, I felt for you in the bed but you weren't there. I guess the kidnapping has affected me more than I thought it had.'

'Don't worry Steve I'm not going anywhere and if anyone feels the need to try again I'll be more prepared than last time. I was stupid, I won't be fooled a second time.'

'You definitely weren't stupid and nobody in the team thinks you were either. You did what you felt was right at the time, we all do it. Sammy's still out there but I have to admit I need a break from chasing him. He's probably out of the country by now making our task much harder.' He reached for his phone to see if he had missed any calls from Port Authorities. Sammy had been on their radar since they realised he was probably the killer who had also kidnapped one of his best officers.

'Why were you out of bed, did something spook you?' asked Steve.

'I've slept so much while I was being held in that metal box, most of the sleep drug induced, I feel tired but I have no desire to go to sleep. I guess my body will catch up with itself in a few days.'

'I'll contact Dave Greenwood and the rest of the team later but I'm going to take a back seat regarding Sammy. My head isn't in the right place. I'm still struggling to think that Sammy is the man responsible for what has happened.'

'Believe me Steve, he is, don't be fooled like I was. He's the killer, he kidnapped me because I got too close to uncovering him. I made the mistake of thinking it couldn't be him. My mistake and mine alone. Don't make the same mistake that I made.'

'I won't, the whole of GMP will know about Sammy by now. Dave can take the lead for a couple of days with John and the rest of the team. If he so much as farts we'll have him.' said Steve.

'I know.'

With that Jude and Steve got back in bed and tried to go back to sleep. It was a while before either of them had calmed their thoughts enough to sleep. When they eventually did wake up they decided to get their walking gear on and decided a walk to Haigh Hall then along the canal and plenty of fresh air was just what they needed to clear their minds.

***

Sammy was due to be moved after two days. During these two days he hadn't eaten anything or drunk anything. He was feeling in a fairly desperate state. His bladder and bowels had shut down because of the lack of sleep and the shock to his system. He had begun to think he would be left to die hanging from a hook in the ceiling. Judging by how he was feeling that wouldn't be too far away. He hadn't seen anyone in the last two days, he had no idea where he was, he had no idea how he had got there. For all he knew he could already be dead and serving his time in hell. If he wasn't dead he certainly felt like it would be preferable to his current position. Just as he was pondering the benefits of his death he heard a lock turn in the door and two men in dark clothes and wearing face covers came into the room. His first thought was that one of the men was built like a man mountain. The other was of average build. The smaller of the two men had a syringe on his hand and wasted no time in getting Sammy sleeping like a baby. Sammy hadn't even tried to speak, he couldn't because he'd been gagged. He was so out of control that he had no choice but to play to the tune the two mismatched men were playing.

When Sammy had been out of it for about a minute the big guy lifted him off the ceiling bracket like he was made out of polystyrene. The man who had used the syringe was cleaning the room behind him, removing a plastic sheet that had covered the floor. His last act in the room had been to pocket the wireless infra-red camera with which they'd been able to keep an eye on Sammy. They knew Sammy would be completely compliant with anything they were about to do to him. Sammy was given no choice in the matter; they were in total control and if they had wanted to kill him they would have done that in his hotel room. That wasn't going to be the outcome today. Today's outcome was delivery of the 'package,' and when the time came, to disappear into the night.

Sammy was bundled into the back of a different van. Again he would recall nothing of the journey. The journey was uneventful, they travelled along a pre-arranged route, this time using only one vehicle and again keeping away from ANPR cameras where possible, sticking within speed limits and giving the police no reason to stop them.

At 3.30am Sammy was delivered. He was taken upstairs and put into a fresh set of pyjamas then into the bed to sleep off the drugs running through his body.

At 3.40am a WhatsApp message was sent to DI Steve Wicks mobile phone from Sammy's mobile phone.

'Steve, I'm tired of playing this game now. It really hasn't worked out the way I wanted it to. I'm giving myself up to you now. I'm back at home, too tired to go on any further on this journey. If you want me I'll be waiting. If you're not here by breakfast I'll take it as a sign and make a run for it. Sammy.'

The smaller of the two men was watching the phone screen. The two ticks came up next to the message within five seconds and waited for the two ticks to turn blue. Thirty seconds later the ticks turned blue. They now knew the message had been read and DI Steve Wicks would be putting things in motion. They knew now he could be here in fifteen minutes if he wanted to be so while the message was being placed the man mountain set up two micro cameras, one to cover the front door and one to cover the back door. They got into the van and drove 300m from Sammy's house and parked up, got in the rear of the van and waited, watching the feeds from front and back doors to see what was going to play out on screen. They wouldn't have long to wait…

***

Jude was still awake when Steve's phone signalled a WhatsApp message. Since the kidnapping she had become hyper sensitive to the any noise but she couldn't get anything other than ten-minute naps during the night. She looked at the clock on the bedside cabinet 3.40am. She thought that was a strange time for anyone to message. She shook Steve awake and told him he had just received a WhatsApp message.

'What did you say?' asked Steve as he was waking up.

'You've just had a WhatsApp message come through on your personal phone and it's 20 to 4 in the morning. It's just come through on your police issued phone too.'

'Whoever it is they're persistent,' replied Steve. He picked up his personal phone and read what had come through. 'You're not going to believe this, it's from Sammy's phone. – 'Steve, I'm tired of playing this game now. It really hasn't worked out the way I wanted it to. I'm giving myself up to you now. I'm back at home, too tired to go on any further on this journey. If you want me I'll be waiting. If you're not here by breakfast I'll take it as a sign and make a run for it. Sammy.'

Steve jumped out of bed and started to get dressed.

'I take it you're going to pick him up…Make sure you have backup…armed backup. He's nothing if not full of surprises, he could be setting you up,' said Jude.

'Absolutely, I'll call for backup on my way. Will you be okay here by yourself?'

'Don't worry about me, I'll lock up when you're out of the door. Go get him Steve. Call me when he's in the cells.'

'I will do, I'd get up if I was you, make yourself a drink, you aren't going to be able to sleep while this is ongoing.'

'I'll be fine,' said Jude, 'go and get the bastard, lock him up, put him behind bars.'

With that Steve was on his way, ringing DCI Dave Greenwood before he was out of the door to tell him what had just happened. John was the next person he rang.

'John, it's Steve, sorry to call you so early but I'm guessing you'll want to be in on this.'

'Guv?'

'Yes John, get yourself dressed and meet me at Sammy's house in Wrightington. I've had a message from Sammy's phone saying he was giving himself up and he was waiting for us there.'

'I'm getting dressed as we speak,' replied John, 'do you think it's genuine?'

'I do, his phone is switched off now so we're going in with armed backup. No nasty surprises with this one we do it by the book. We've seen what he's capable of, double murderer, kidnapping a police officer and maybe other historic offences. Still hard to believe in my head but we'll not be fooled twice.'

'I'll be there in no time.'

'Good lad. I'll be parked up on the road, waiting for backup.' Steve knew he could count on John, even in the middle of the night

Steve was thinking that things didn't happen like this, nothing like this had ever happened to him before. It all seemed too easy for a criminal. Why hadn't he just handed himself in at his nearest police station. Sammy was flamboyant and nothing should surprise him about this case. The next thought that came to him was that it might be a setup and he might want to kidnap Jude again as his bargaining chip. 'Steve…pull yourself together man,' he thought. It didn't stop him ringing Jude though. He got a shock when Angie answered.

'Hello Steve, Jude has just told me what has happened, she's in the kitchen putting the kettle on. Myself and Jamie have just got back from London, we've got news and we wanted you two to be the first to hear it. We decided to come here and sleep until you were both up. We would have been here earlier had it not been for a tree having been blown down across the line just past Birmingham.' Said Angie. As long as nobody checked on train disruptions outside Birmingham there would be no questions calling in to doubt why they turned up at Steve's at 3.50 in the morning.

'Angie, I'm so glad you're there, crazy thoughts going through my mind…'

'Jude's fine Steve, she was watching tv when we came in, drinking hot chocolate. She's safer than you could imagine. Don't worry, we'll speak later. She's just doing toast; we all became suddenly very hungry.'

'Okay Angie, I'll let you know what's happened when it's happened.'

Steve cut the call, happy that Jude was safe. He was hoping the need to wrap her in cotton wool wasn't going to last too long. He'd forgotten already about Angie's news. More important things to see to first going on in his world right now.

Steve was first to arrive. It was only knowing that this could be a setup that stopped him going in without waiting for backup. If it was a hoax he could live with that, there was always another day. If it was a trap there might never be another day…without backup. At that moment, sat in his car with the heater on full because the sky was clear and frost was all over the roads, pavements and trees, he knew that his life with Jude excited him more than he'd felt since the day his daughter was born. Before he could do anything about his feelings he had a killer to bring in, without any further deaths. He needed to hear what Sammy had to say, why he'd felt the need to do what he'd done. He'd been a good man, one of the best in Steve's mind. If it hadn't been for Jude's tenacity he might be still flying under the radar, having slipped out of the country on his own terms.

John was next to show up, parking behind Steve. John opened Steve's passenger door and got in.

'No backup yet guv?'

'They'll be here shortly.'

'Sammy's house looks dark. If I remember correctly, his living room and his bedroom are at the back of the house.'

'There are a few ways this could unfold as I see it. Firstly, the message was a hoax. Sammy giving us the finger for having found Jude. When we go in he'll be nowhere to be found. Secondly, he's in there ready to hand himself over to us, none violently. Thirdly, he's in there but has decided he's going down with a fight. I don't believe that's the case; Sammy must know we'll be going in safe on this one and if he wants a gunfight he'll be dead before he hits the floor. I don't think Sammy is stupid enough to think he could win on this one. I could be wrong though; he's had a long time to think things through.'

'Who knows what's going on in his head,' replied John, 'a couple of weeks ago we knew nothing about the murders and if you'd asked me, when Sammy was at Greenacres giving us his initial findings, if the guy who was talking to us could have been the murderer I would have said definitely not.'

'Me too John, and we'd both be wrong.'

Just then two cars pulled up behind John's car. six officers got out in body armour. They each carried a Heckler & Koch G36 5.56mm assault rifle and a holstered Walther P99 semi-automatic pistol. Steve and John got their body armour out of the boots of their cars even though they wouldn't be entering the house until given the all clear by the armed officers.

Steve discussed with the lead armed officer and his team, telling them how they found themselves in this position so early on a very cold morning. None of the eight officers were feeling the cold though, the adrenaline was flowing through their bodies with the anticipation of the job to come.

'We force entry into the house, it's a big house five bedrooms, living room, dining room, kitchen, utility room, three bathrooms a large garage and about an acre of grounds. If he's here he'll probably come quickly but let's not expect that. He's killed already and he may kill again.'

'Okay, DI Wicks, we'll go in three men around the back, three men in front. The back door team will cover the downstairs, the front door team will cover upstairs. Myself and officers Grey and Daniels and will cover upstairs, officers Long, Cooke and Asson will cover downstairs. We'll tell you when it's safe to enter, do not enter until we give you the all clear. If we find him we'll hold him until the rest of the house is cleared.'

'Thanks, Keith, you're in charge of this stage, I'll wait at the front door, DS Pace will be at the back.'

'Okay guys, let's get in place and we go on my call.'

Twenty seconds later the call was given and the six-armed officers went to work, fully committed as far as the task in hand was concerned. It was the only way to be if you wanted to still be breathing at the end of the day.

After about a minute the all clear was given and the lead armed officer called for Steve and John to join him upstairs.

'Is this target DI Wicks?'

'It is.'

'He was lay on the bed, looked like he'd nodded off waiting for us…would you believe it.'

'Steve?' said Sammy, looking bewildered, 'Where am I, what's just happened?'

Steve had no desire to play along with whatever Sammy thought he was doing. 'Make the arrest John, I'll get a unit here to take him in.'

Sammy was silent, he didn't understand what had just happened. He knew that the game was over, he just didn't understand how it had happened.

'Samuel David Lomas, you are under arrest for two cases of murder and the kidnap of a police officer. You do not have to say anything, but it may harm your defence if you do not mention when questioned something you may later rely on in court. Anything you do say may be given in evidence.'

Sammy, still looking confused was handcuffed and lead downstairs to await the police van to arrive and take him to the station for questioning.

'John, can you take care of things here and get him over to the station and make sure he's in a cell?' asked Steve. 'I've got no desire to have any interaction with him at this time. I need to get home. We'll pick things up tomorrow.'

'Yes guv, of course, I'll handle it from here and we'll get some answers tomorrow… actually, later today.'

'Thanks John, see you in a few hours.'

Steve had no desire to speak to Sammy at this time in the morning. He'd speak to Sammy when they had him in custody. For now he wanted to speak to Jude, reassure her that it was all over and Sammy would probably be spending the rest of his life at his Majesty's pleasure.

Chapter Twenty-Six

Two weeks later
The sun was shining on Wigan for the first time in what felt like an age. To Steve it seemed like the Gods were making sure the funeral went ahead without a hitch. There was a very good turnout, Ruth Wicks had lots of friends and close neighbours. She would have been pleased to see the Crematorium had standing room only for any late comers. There was a get together later at the Boar's Head, large wooden beams and very atmospheric, just down the road from Steve's apartment. Ruth loved this pub when she was alive, it felt very correct that after her death they'd celebrate her life, say goodbye to her and help those left behind to move forward.

In the pub the topic quickly, among the colleagues who had come to support Steve, become about Sammy. There was only so much consideration you can show at a funeral before things became about more every day issues. There were many people there who wanted to know what the latest news was on Sammy. The local news channels and media had latched onto the murders and kidnapping. Having a prominent figure from within the Wigan community being held was definitely newsworthy, particularly as he appeared to be such a popular and some would say outstanding figure.

'What's the latest on Sammy?' asked Jamie, 'He's certainly caught the nations morbid attention, he'll end up going down as part of Wigan's history that Wigan would rather forget.'

'It's been very easy Jamie; he's confessed to the two murders and Jude's kidnapping. He's been singing like a bird, accepted more or less immediately that he is guilty on both counts of murder and kidnapping Jude. We found the murder weapon where Jude was being held, very much like a medieval war hammer. It turned out Sammy is a half-decent welder to add to his long list of abilities. His defence will likely be looking at a plea of insanity,' replied Steve, 'the onus is on his defence council to prove it. I just don't see Sammy wanting to be shown as insane. Having said that I also wouldn't have believed he was capable of murdering two people.'

'From what Angie tells me, so far he's made decisions to act in the way he did long before he played those decisions out. He even manufactured the murder weapon specifically to make an enormous amount of damage. If that's not pre-planning I don't know what is.' Said Jamie.

'He can afford the best when it comes to arguing his case. He'll spend the rest of his life behind bars, you can be assured of that. It will be either in a prison or a secure mental health unit such as Ashworth. I'm not bothered one way or the other, either way he'll never feel the freedom we all take for granted again. How are things coming along with setting up a security business out of nothing?'

'Slowly,' Jamie replied, 'but it's what we expected, to be fair. Between myself and Angie we've got more than enough contacts and experience, we just haven't owned and run an independent security business, yet. There are a lot of jobs we could get involved in within the Middle East, highly funded and if you know your stuff, relatively safe. Fortunately we do know our stuff.'

'Sounds exciting, I'm sure there must be some big holes you could fall into unless you know what you're doing.'

'Very much so, but to put your mind at rest myself and especially Angie will be operating mainly in the UK in a consultancy role. We may travel to dangerous countries but we'll have our own security and even then we'll be in and out quickly, we'll write our report with expert recommendations and be back in the UK before you know we're gone.'

'Good to know.'

'There are some very rich people out there whose wealth attracts the wrong sort of attention. They feel the need to surround themselves against danger. That's where we come in and luckily for us there are a whole lot of dangerous people out there too.'

'Don't I know it. Some dangerous people are far too close to home for my liking.'

'Well Steve, the world has one less dangerous man with a screw loose to worry about thanks to you and your team.'

'You could say that, but I'm not quite sure how it happened the way it did. Sammy swears he doesn't know how he ended up in his bedroom at the time he did and where he came from before that. He's definitely missing a part of his memory. To be honest I'm not that concerned about that, he's locked up and will never see the light of day again, apart from an hour to exercise every day if he's lucky. He's committed his last murder unless he commits one on the inside. I think his murdering days are over though.' Said Steve, 'His get away planning was fairly half-hearted although there are two very expensive cars currently on their way to Cuba. So we know there was some planning, we just haven't got anything like a full picture yet.'

'What made him do what he did?' Jamie asked.

'I think that's the easiest question to answer. He lost the two most important people in his life in fairly quick succession. On the outside he seemed okay, some people can hide their feelings very well, others wear their hearts on their sleeves. Sammy could hide his true feelings very well while planning revenge. Revenge for his cousin's murder, the man he looked up to from a very early age. The other person he lost was Jane, the person who was bringing real meaning to his life. He was feeling like the luckiest person in the world. Jane was, according to Sammy his soulmate…but then she died too. Up until she was diagnosed with incurable lung cancer his life was everything he desired it to be. When she died it meant that a life for a life was well and truly back on the table, and he had someone he could blame for that, the man who helped put his cousin behind bars. He couldn't blame anyone for Jane's death but he still held onto the bile regarding his cousin.'

'It's a sad thing but 999 times out of 1000 it wouldn't even cross a person's mind.'

'You're right of course. I also believe that tragically losing the two most important people in your world could easily tip the balance and the law is the law, I'm sure you understand that Jamie.'

'Unfortunately more than most. Myself and Angie have walked the fine line between legal and illegal for queen and country, and lately king and country. We've done it with the security of our country in mind. I'm sure you understand that too Steve.'

'I do Jamie, and for that I'm very grateful to you both. However Sammy came to be in the place he did at that time he didn't do it without some outside help. We both understand I'll never get to know the truth of it but we got the right result and that was very important.'

'We understand each other really well Steve. Sometimes it's the result that counts rather than knowing the ins and outs of the journey that was taken to get there.'

***

Back at the apartment Steve and Jude were shattered. Funerals were never events where you could fully enjoy the day. It's a time when the most you can get out of it is the pleasure of knowing that you played your part in it and it went without a hitch. Steve felt it was a necessary act to enable him to move forward.

His mother's assets were being sorted out by himself and Angie. Work on Sammy's case was continuing slowly but Steve felt like getting to a quick conclusion was what he should be working on. Jude was due to go back to work tomorrow having been seen by the work psychologist and put on temporary light duties after the trauma. Things for Steve were going well and the earlier conversation with Jamie was something he accepted and would never speak of again.

'Steve, I've got something to tell you and I'm hoping you're going to be okay with it. I waited until after your Mum's funeral to bring it up.' Said Jude.

'Sounds ominous.' Steve stretched his arms above his head when he was tired and that was where his hands were when Jude spoke again.

'I'm pregnant, I know it's a shock and I would have liked to have planned it…Steve put your arms down, you look like a chimpanzee with your arms above your head. Say something.'

Steve lowered his arms down.

'I wasn't expecting that…just give me a minute will you.'

Steve walked through to the kitchen and could be heard fumbling in the cupboards while Jude was thinking the worst. After what felt like five minutes but what could only have been a matter of ten seconds he walked back into the lounge carrying a bottle of champagne and two glasses.

'Jude, I couldn't be more pleased. I never could have imagined how I'd feel after the car crash wiped out my precious girls but this feels right. I didn't know if I could ever handle a situation like that again so I pushed it to a place where I rarely go if I can help it, and if I did my head was filled what ifs and buts. Now it's happened it feels just right.'

'Oh Steve, I've been so worried about telling you, I won't lie,' said Jude, 'I'm ready for motherhood, I'm having feelings I've never felt before. I know it wasn't planned but I'm not sure either of us could've been part of the planning process; I think this is probably the only way we would have come to this point. Does that make sense?'

Steve took Jude in his arms and all the tension drained from her body.

'It does, Jude, don't worry I'm fully committed to us and whatever we bring into this world. You'll make a fantastic mum Jude. This is the best news we could have; it feels like a new beginning on the day we said goodbye to my mum. I love you Jude.'

'I love you too.'

The End

Acknowledgements

My sister, Sandra, really needs to be acknowledged for her help, every step of the way, giving encouragement and suggestions. My good friend Wendy has also given me great encouragement.

I have to mention the place where all this started. Greenacres, in the book, is loosely based on Greengrass Community Centre in Hag Fold, Wigan. Greengrass plays an important role in the lives of so many. Lynn and Laura welcomed me in and it is where a great deal of this book was written. I would also like to thank the dedicated band of volunteers, without whom the centre couldn't run and who kept me supplied with copious amounts of coffee during the process. Keep the kettle going folks, now for book two in the series.

THANKS TO YOU ALL FOR READING.